BIT OF A SCUFFLE IN THE CHAPEL

Miss Seeton's musings were disturbed by a muffled clanking noise, and for the first time she experienced a flicker of unease. She pointed her torch toward the vestry, the door of which she then saw was ajar . . .

Having left the church door open, she had not heard William Parsons enter behind her. Parsons himself was in a state of indecision. He had been given no instructions as to what he should do if he saw, while his colleagues in crime were about their business, a slightly built, elderly lady approach and make for the church door. Something had to be done, though, so he had quietly followed her—and temporarily he had lost his head and pounced when she had called out. With his hand now clamped firmly over her mouth, he could keep the old girl reasonably quiet, but that left only one of his arms free to control her furious and surprisingly agile struggles . . .

Heron Carvic's Miss Seeton Books
From The Berkley Publishing Group

ADVANTAGE MISS SEETON
MISS SEETON, BY APPOINTMENT
MISS SEETON DRAWS THE LINE
MISS SEETON SINGS
ODDS ON MISS SEETON
PICTURE MISS SEETON
WITCH MISS SEETON

ADVANTAGE MISS SEETON

HAMPTON CHARLES

BERKLEY BOOKS, NEW YORK

ADVANTAGE MISS SEETON

A Berkley Book / published by arrangement with
the author

PRINTING HISTORY
Berkley edition / June 1990

For information address: The Berkley Publishing Group,
200 Madison Avenue, New York, New York 10016.

ISBN: 0-425-12237-9

A BERKLEY BOOK® TM 757,375
Berkley Books are published by The Berkley Publishing Group,
200 Madison Avenue, New York, New York 10016.
The name "BERKLEY" and the "B" logo
are trademarks belonging to Berkley Publishing Corporation.

PRINTED IN THE UNITED STATES OF AMERICA

10 9 8 7 6 5 4 3 2 1

For Melinda Metz,
and with a respectful nod and wink
to the shade of Heron Carvic

chapter
–1–

"DON'T *do* THAT!" Thrudd Banner yelped as his companion dug her elbow into his ribs. "If you make me drop this lens I swear I'll send you the bill for a new one. I'm a freelancer, remember? Have to pay for my own gear?" In his agitation he had to make two attempts before succeeding in getting the telephoto lens to click into place.

Far from apologizing, Amelita Forby of the *Daily Negative* slowly and deliberately repeated the offense. "Pay attention when I poke you, buster," she said. "Or I may go poke somebody more receptive. Look over there. See what I see?"

The gesture she made with her right index finger was hardly perceptible, but it was clear enough to Thrudd, who glanced in the direction indicated. His eyes flickered from side to side for a second or two. Then he sat very still, and a smile gradually replaced his look of irritation. "Well, I'll go to the foot of our stairs!" he murmured eventually. "Miss Emily D. Seeton, as I live and breathe. Now what in the world is she doing here, d'you reckon? And the others? Some kind of a parish outing? That's the vicar, I can tell by his dog collar."

Mel favored him with a parody of an adoring smile and

fluttered her eyelashes. "Gosh, you're so *brilliant*. It's the way you seize on these practically imperceptible clues that gets me. By crikey, you have to get up early in the morning to hoodwink Scoop Banner, the journo with the X-ray eyes!"

"Shut up," Thrudd suggested genially. "Don't think they've spotted us yet, too many other rubberneckers milling about. Do we go over and say hello, or what?"

"Not yet." Grasping him firmly by one forearm, Mel towed him out of sight behind a convenient tree. "I've got a better idea. They're heading for the temporary seating. In a minute we'll nip round the back and get into the scaffolding frame underneath them. Because what we're going to do is eavesdrop. I feel a delightful little vignette for the Saturday edition coming on. Along the lines of a much-praised piece I did last month about minor country gentry up for the Chelsea Flower Show. This way I'll be able to lace it with authentic dialogue."

Thrudd pulled a face. "Not sure that's quite fair, Mel. They're by way of being friends of ours, and, well, it might be a private conversation—"

"Private codswallop! People don't come and sit in a crowd to watch two top women tennis players and then get involved in a private conversation. Politely goofy nonsense is what I'm after, and take it from me, that's all there'll be on offer."

Nigel Colveden was the effective shepherd of the little flock from Plummergen in Kent, and he was taking his responsibilities as seriously as his enraptured state permitted. In practice this meant that from time to time he turned, beaming fatuously, to make sure that the Reverend Arthur Treeves, Miss Molly Treeves, and Miss Emily Seeton were following him into the extra banks of seating which had been squeezed into the confines of the principal tennis court to accommodate as many spectators as possible. It was a lovely afternoon, and though the streets of London were hot, dusty, and smelled of exhaust fumes, the spacious grounds of the Hurlingham Club were, as the vicar had just aptly put it, a veritable *rus in urbe*.

The prospect of watching some world-class tennis had drawn a considerable crowd, but was nevertheless far from dominating the consciousness of any one of the Plummergen quartet. Nigel himself had little interest in the game for its own sake, but was deeply in love with the rising young English star Trish Thumper, who was due to begin a singles match against the formidable American Nancy Wiesendonck at two-thirty.

Nigel had recognized the truth about his feelings at four fifty-three in the afternoon of the Thursday of the previous week, about an hour and twenty minutes after meeting Trish for the first time. Being young, chivalrous, and naive, he attributed his present euphoria simply to the delightful awareness that he would in a few minutes be able to feast his eyes on his beloved again. The less ethereal thought that she would on this occasion be wearing a tennis dress so short that it would permit frequent glimpses of what could well turn out to be frilly panties underneath was buried deep in his subconscious mind.

Miss Molly Treeves was recapitulating in her mind the arguments Mrs. Skinner had deployed that morning in support of her contention that it was Mrs. Henderson's turn to see to the flowers in church three Sundays hence and not hers, and her own brisk demolition of Mrs. Skinner's case. Her satisfaction was marred only by a nagging uncertainty as to whether she had remembered to switch off the electric iron before leaving the vicarage.

Her brother, having contributed his thoughts on the subject of the attractions of the lawns and pleasances provided for the delectation of members of the Hurlingham Club and their guests, had retreated into a reverie about the Pelagian heresy, his favorite. Mr. Treeves thought he could very probably come to some sort of conscientious arrangement with Pelagianism, but doubted if his own circumstances were such that it was technically possible for him to become a heretic.

The go-ahead Suffragan Bishop of Greenwich had quite recently stressed, not for the first time, that whatever an ordained priest's state of mind he remained a bona fide clerk in Holy Orders, but Mr. Treeves remained unconvinced. For he had woken up one morning some years earlier to the realization that his trouble wasn't so much a matter of problems with a few of the Thirty-Nine Articles as of not believing a single word of the whole kit and caboodle of Christianity. It was confusing therefore that nobody except himself seemed to care. The bishop seemed quite unconcerned, none of the parishioners in Plummergen appeared to have noticed anything amiss, and Molly, in whom he had on one occasion timidly confided, had simply snorted and told him to pull himself together and fetch a jar of bottled greengages from the larder.

Compared with those of her companions, Miss Seeton's thoughts were on a lower plane altogether. She was certainly not in love. In her young days there had been times when Cupid had taken aim at her heart, and she cherished a few tender and very private memories which just now and then she retrieved and, as it were, lovingly dusted off and polished. So she could understand and sympathize with the personal problems of others, but it had been many years since she had last experienced emotional perturbation on her own account.

Nor was she troubled by religious doubts. Her occasional

participation in the rites and ceremonies of the Church of England was for Miss Seeton a matter of good manners, involving neither intellectual conundrums nor crises of conscience. Unlike Mrs. Skinner, she neither knew nor cared when it was her turn to do the flowers in the church, but simply buckled to whenever so instructed by Miss Treeves.

Finally, and thanks to Mrs. Martha Bloomer who did for her so splendidly, Miss Seeton never had to ask herself whether she had inadvertently left the oven or the electric iron on. What Miss Seeton was in fact wondering, as she made her way to the seat indicated by Nigel Colveden, was why her valued friends and resourceful allies Miss Forby and Mr. Banner had crept away and concealed themselves behind a tree, in what could only be thought of as a surreptitious manner. A serene little smile on her face, she pondered possible explanations for their odd behavior.

Mr. Banner and Miss Forby were, of course, important and busy people who each no doubt had professional reasons to be at the Hurlingham Club: Mr. Banner to concern himself with the foreigners, and Miss Forby perhaps to interview one or another of the famous women players involved in exhibition matches that day. It might well be that their time was at such a premium that they could not afford to stand and chat, and that they had therefore decided it would be the courteous thing to pretend not to have seen her.

Yes, that was the most likely thing. Nigel had explained on the train from Brettenden—so kind of Lady Colveden to have driven them all to the station from Plummergen—that both Nancy Wiesendonck and her English rival were currently the object of a great deal of press interest. As presumably were others of the contenders due to participate in the Wimbledon championship matches later in the month.

Dear Nigel, such a susceptible boy, had spoken almost exclusively about Trish Thumper, and had no idea whether or not her opponent owed her unusual surname to some family connection with the Mathilde Wesendonk who had been Richard Wagner's . . . well, friend. And Miss Thumper was undoubtedly a fine, healthy young woman, in spite of the fact that neither of her parents seemed to be blessed with robust constitutions. But then the atmosphere in the Old Bailey was probably far from salubrious, and Sir Wilfred very likely picked up all manner of mild infections there and passed them on to his wife.

Mr. Justice Thumper. What an unfortunate name . . . and oh dear, how silly one had been as a child, imagining that senior judges just happened all to have been given the uplifting Christian name "Justice" when they were babies, rather as girls of earlier generations had been called Mercy, or Charity. And that if a little boy's name was Justice he might well grow up with the idea of studying the law rather than wishing to become an engine driver or a fireman. But then one had been confused by so many things at that age, innocently wondering for example why so many journalists became involved in divorce cases, because all the men who behaved badly seemed to be described in the newspapers as "corespondents".

"I'm so sorry, Vicar. I was daydreaming and didn't quite catch what you said."

Seated on Miss Seeton's right, Mr. Treeves smiled at her with pleasure. He was so often in a similar position vis-a-vis his sister Molly, and it was comforting to encounter a kindred spirit.

"It is I who should apologize, for having disturbed you. I merely wished to point out that Sir Wilfred and Lady Thumper have just arrived. They are seated two, no, three rows below us, and some distance away to our left. How kind it was of the Colvedens to invite us to tea to meet them last week. And, of course, their gifted and charming daughter Patricia who so generously provided our tickets for today. We should on this occasion refer to her by her professional name, I suppose, though I take leave to doubt whether Sir Wilfred would think it desirable." The vicar sighed enviously. "It is rare to encounter a man of such, er, firm principles."

"Indeed it is. One feels confident that he enjoys his work."

"And he and Sir George have been friends since boyhood, it seems. Former schoolmates who have both achieved distinction in their respective walks of life. In fact, I gathered from their conversation that the judge is the younger of the two. By three or four years, and that he had to perform various menial tasks for his senior. Making his toast, cleaning his shoes, and so on."

"Fag!" Miss Seeton announced unexpectedly and in a clear, carrying voice just as Mel Forby and Thrudd Banner arrived underneath her. "That is the word I have been searching for. Imagine the dignified and unbending Mr. Justice Thumper being a fag, Vicar. Can you credit it?"

"It does require a considerable effort of the imagination, certainly. But I assure you that I have it on Sir George Colveden's own authority . . ."

The rest of whatever Mr. Treeves had to say was lost in a great surge of applause as the players entered the court. Mel and Thrudd gaped at each other in silent stupefaction for several seconds, and then picked their way out of the forest of scaffolding. Thrudd was the first to recover the power of speech. "You did hear what I heard? Miss S. and the vicar agreeing that Trish Thumper's old man's a fag?"

"That's what I heard all right." Amelita (née Amelia) Forby was a native of Liverpool, and a child of the people. She had learned a great deal about the ways of the upper classes since becoming first a fashion writer and in more recent years the *Daily Negative*'s star woman columnist, but was too young to have heard of the defunct fagging system which formerly prevailed in most of England's great boarding schools.

So was Thrudd Banner, to whom also the word "fag" meant only one thing. Well, two actually, because he remembered his father using it to mean a cheap cigarette. "Good grief. What was that you said about politely goofy nonsense? You sure as hell won't be able to use that fragment of dialogue in your column, sweetheart. Old Thumper's the most notorious old brute in the business."

This was true. Mr. Justice Thumper was what until the abolition—which he deplored—of capital punishment had been called a hanging judge. His homilies from the bench were of a moral severity that might have been thought extreme even by a congregation listening in the kirk to a sermon by an unusually dour Scottish preacher. His Lordship did not when passing sentence on those found guilty refer explicitly to hell and damnation, but sensitive persons present in court tended to sniff the air uneasily as if to catch the odor of brimstone.

It occasionally happened that in spite of the judge's frequent acid interventions, defense counsel managed to persuade a jury that the accused was innocent. In such cases Mr. Justice Thumper had no option but to discharge the prisoner from the dock, but in doing so he generally contrived to imply that there was no smoke without fire, and that whatever the jurors had decided, the person before him was a pretty miserable specimen anyway who ought to pull himself together.

For these reasons, Sir Wilfred Thumper was a man the popular newspapers loved to hate, and they reported his more colorful remarks with zest. "Thumper Flays Do-Gooders," a headline might shriek, or "Jail These Welfare

Fiddlers, Says Judge.'' So long as his talented daughter Patricia was just one among dozens of young tennis hopefuls, she escaped the attentions of the press, but by the time she was fifteen she had emerged from the ruck as a junior champion. Her wicked backhand was her particular strength, and she was being admiringly referred to in the sports pages as ''Trish The Tigress'' or simply ''The Young Thumper.'' Now that she was at nineteen being tipped as the girl who might within a few years upset the likes of Ann Jones or even Billie Jean King, sports writers and subeditors were vying with each other in making bad puns on her name and the notorious reputation of her eminent father.

Mel Forby and Thrudd Banner stayed where they were and went on discussing the overheard exchange between Miss Seeton and the vicar for some minutes. Other people were coming and going behind the bank of temporary seating, because Trish Thumper and Nancy Wiesendonck were warming up and the match proper had yet to begin. They had therefore no reason to suppose that they were making themselves conspicuous, or objects of interest. Neither of them noticed the wiry, ferret-faced man nearby who seemed to be having trouble with one of his shoelaces.

chapter

~2~

"OH, THE usual I should imagine, sir. All the works that are done under the sun, as Ecclesiastes so neatly put it. And the sun does have a habit of reporting for duty during Wimbledon fortnight. Ticket touts, pickpockets, dirty old men touching up young girls in the crowd. Vanity and vexation of spirit enough, but nothing the local divisional chaps haven't had plenty of practice in handling over the years."

As he spoke, Chief Superintendent Delphick studied his superior's expression with care. It wasn't like the Assistant Commissioner (Crime) to concern himself personally with the grubby froth of petty villainy that washed about the edges of the sea of serious illegality they normally spent their time charting.

"Quite," Sir Hubert Everleigh said, a little testily because he envied The Oracle his apparently effortless skill in producing apt quotations. "What about the VIPs, though? How much thought's given to their security?"

"With respect, sir, you're almost certainly better informed than I am about that. The duke of Kent'll no doubt attend several times, being the new president, and presumably he'll have the usual protection. As will the duchess and any other royals or top politicians who decide to go."

"Yes, yes, of course, that goes without saying. Wasn't thinking about them, though. The players, Delphick. Since they let the professionals in and started offering prize money a couple of years back, the whole thing has become—"

"A different ball game, sir?"

"Don't try me too far, Chief Superintendent." Everleigh harrumphed to disguise a chuckle. "But as a matter of fact, that's literally true. Some of the participants are now very valuable in the strict financial sense. Like racehorses. And people do gamble on the results. Might occur to somebody to try to nobble a fancied contender. Or kidnap one."

Delphick was impressed. The thought had not previously entered his head, and he had to admit that old Sir Heavily had a point. "That's a solemn thought, sir. Though I'm bound to say that any misguided kidnapper who tried to snatch Rod Laver or Ken Rosewall would probably get more than he bargained for. The women on the other hand . . ."

"Precisely. No doubt they're well chaperoned while they're on Wimbledon premises, as it were, but they come and go pretty casually most of the time. Well, no point in my going on beating about the bush. Fact is, we might have a specific problem on our hands this year. Does the name Trish Thumper mean anything to you?"

"Yes indeed. My wife tells me she's a young lady to watch. And she's the daughter of the judge, of course."

"Yes. I've met him now and then, and entre nous, I cordially dislike the man. Known among barristers as Thump the Grump, I'm told. Seems to model himself on Judge Jeffreys of infamous memory. D'you know he was blackballed when he was up for election to the Garrick?" The assistant commissioner cast a smug glance down at the pale green and pink stripes of his club necktie, and Delphick toyed with the idea that it might have been Sir Hubert himself who had given the thumbs down. "Anyway, it seems he's been getting threatening letters."

"I'm not a bit surprised, sir. There must be any number of people he's sent down who'd cheerfully murder him if they thought they could get away with it. I infer from what you say that the threats are directed at his daughter, though."

"Precisely. Us coppers have to get used to threats from disgruntled villains or their friends and relatives, and so do judges. Even judges who don't browbeat and throw the book at the people they put away with such obvious relish as Wilfred Thumper." Sir Hubert got up, crossed to the window of his office, and peered out for a while before wheeling round and marching back to his chair again. "So in the ordinary way we wouldn't lose a lot of sleep over Thumper's hate mail, but this is something different. You're not the only one who remembers bits from the Bible, you know. There's something about visiting the sins of the fathers on the child unto the . . . how many generations is it, Delphick?"

"Seven, I fancy."

"Probably. However many it is, it's a jolly unfair principle, and not one supported by the commissioner or myself. With a father like that, Miss Patricia Thumper probably has quite enough to put up with as it is. If somebody out there's harboring evil designs on her, we've got to look into it. What I mean by that, of course, is that *you've* got to look into it." Sir Hubert pushed a slender file across his desk toward Delphick.

"This is all the paper work there is so far. Thumper raised the matter personally with the commissioner, at the suggestion of your old acquaintance Sir George Colveden."

"*Colveden*, sir?"

"The same. Apparently they've kept in touch since they were at school together, and Colveden, it seems, though a mere justice of the peace, is the only man on earth whose opinions Mr. Justice Thumper respects."

"Good lord!"

"My sentiments entirely. Now the commissioner isn't any fonder of the odious man than I am. Nevertheless he tells me that although you'd have to squeeze long and hard to extract so much as a drop of the milk of human kindness from him, it's there. It seems that Mr. Justice Thumper loves his daughter with all of what passes for his heart, and would probably go out of his mind if anything were to happen to her."

In his ecstasy Nigel Colveden seized a hand conveniently near his and clasped it tightly. It belonged to Miss Treeves, who was startled and gratified in about equal measure. Trish Thumper had lost the first set to the American girl two–six, but succeeded in taking the second, six–four. "Isn't she fantastic?" he demanded.

Miss Treeves gazed down to where the two young women sat below the umpire's elevated chair, mopping their faces with towels and drinking Coca-Cola. "They are well matched," she said, decisively disengaging her hand, "but if, as I imagine, you are referring to Trish Thumper, then Arthur and I agree that she seems to have the greater stamina and will probably win."

"Oh, rather!" The vicar had long ago learned not to challenge the opinions his sister attributed to him. He turned to Miss Seeton with the idea of inviting her to make the decision unanimous, but she was obviously lost in thought, so he left her undisturbed.

The Thumper parents were both gazing at their daughter, their heads turned in such a way that Miss Seeton had a clear view of Sir Wilfred in profile. Lady Thumper was on his far side and largely obscured by her husband. She was in any case wearing a huge and elaborate hat that for some reason put Miss Seeton in mind of the Taj Mahal and would in any case have largely concealed her expression from anyone behind and above her.

It was of little consequence, Miss Seeton thought to herself, remembering tea at the Colvedens. Poor Lady Thumper must presumably in her youth have made an impression on the man who was to become her husband, but in late middle age seemed to have no personality whatever of her own. One would be hard put to it indeed to catch any kind of likeness on paper.

Sir Wilfred's face on the other hand was both memorable and expressive of oddly contradictory traits of character. In fact, now that one thought about it, he looked very like Leonardo Loredan, the doge of Venice in Bellini's wonderful portrait. He had the same ascetic air of authority, a similarly proud, prominent nose, and thin lips pressed together just as censoriously. Hundreds of years ago this doge too must surely have struck many of his acquaintances as being a querulous, opinionated, and self-righteous person. And the doges were elected from men who had earlier in their careers sat in judgment in the Venetian court of law, of course. So it was not at all fanciful to suppose that Leonardo, like Sir Wilfred, had earned a reputation for severity. Yet Bellini's portrait showed a man whose eyes betrayed vulnerability and even pain; and there had been a kindred look in Sir Wilfred's whenever his face had been turned toward his only child while they had all been sitting there on the terrace at Rytham Hall having tea. Quite different from when he had been talking to Sir George, for whom he clearly had much respect, but that was perhaps only to be expected if their relationship as boys had been as the vicar had explained.

"I wonder if they had lemon curd at school?"

"Did you say lemon curd, Miss Seeton?" His attention being on the players who were on the point of beginning the third set, the vicar was not sure if he had heard aright.

"Yes. It was a great treat to have it at the Colvedens last week, I can't imagine why it seems to have gone so much out of fashion in recent years. Perhaps Sir George asked specially for it because he remembered it was a favorite of Sir Wilfred's all those years ago. He's very like Bellini's doge, don't you think?"

Arthur Treeves looked at her uneasily but was spared the necessity to make an immediate reply as a hush fell and Trish Thumper prepared to serve. Nigel Colveden barely managed to suppress a moan of yearning when she swung her racket, the material of her dress taut across her considerable bosom and the scalloped skirt rising up her well-muscled thighs. It was a good service, but Nancy Wiesendonck returned it deftly. The rally ran to several exchanges, but the Thumper backhand eventually prevailed. Fifteen–love.

"Bellini's dogs?" The vicar turned to inquire during the burst of applause. "I don't think I know anyone of that name. Not who keeps dogs, that is," he added, as though he had any number of other Bellini acquaintances. He was immediately shushed by his sister, smiled apologetically at Miss Seeton, and remained silent until the end of the first game, which Trish Thumper won. By then, he could see that Miss Seeton had in any case fallen into another reverie, so he beamed across at Nigel. "How well she is playing!"

Miss Seeton blinked, rubbed her eyes, and blinked again. Most of the heads of the spectators turned from left to right to follow the ball, but the doge of Venice's gaze never left his daughter. While, how very interesting, somebody was staring equally fixedly at the doge. No less a person than Tintoretto, who was in St. John's Ambulance Brigade uniform and standing by the fence behind the base line at the end currently occupied by Trish Thumper. Come now, one really must not carry fantasy to the point of self-indulgence: It was merely that Sir Wilfred *looked* like the doge, and the first-aid man *looked* like Tintoretto in his self-portrait, his cadaverous, tragic face given a false appearance of fullness by the huge, untidy gray beard.

It was the first time that William Parsons had worn his old uniform in public for nearly six years. He had lost weight in prison and it felt loose and heavy on him; but he was confident that it would pass muster. In the old days he had more than once joked that the Red Cross and St. John's volunteers at concerts and sporting occasions were Invisible People, like the postman in the detective story. Seen by everybody, noticed by nobody. And even if they had heard it before, Audrey and Vicky had laughed, affectionately he believed.

For they had been a better-than-averagely contented, united little family in those days. To have risen to be the manager of the busy branch of the Reliable Building Society in Streatham High Street might not amount to the career success William had once daydreamed about, but it was nothing to be ashamed of. The salary was adequate if hardly generous, and as a member of the managerial staff he was charged an exceptionally low rate of interest on the mortgage repayments for their own house. On the whole he enjoyed interviewing young couples wanting loans to enable them to set up their own homes, and the staff of the branch worked together pretty well as a team. So he hardly ever went home having had a "bad day at the office."

Audrey used to tease him about the amount of his spare time he devoted to the St. John's Ambulance Brigade. "You're a fanatic, that's what you are, Albert Schweitzer," she would say as he got ready to report for duty at a Saturday football match. "Why, you don't even like football." Then, when he thought he sensed real resentment underlying the breeziness and hesitated, "Go on, get along with you, you daft thing. Enjoy yourself. Hope you have something a bit more interesting than a sprained ankle this week."

There was no such ambiguity about Vicky's attitude. She idolized her father, and joined the brigade, too, as a cadet, as soon as she was old enough. From then on they were not only father and daughter, but colleagues and allies, too. William was proud of the bright, pretty teenager he had for a daughter, and Vicky confided in him in a way she could never bring herself to do with her mother.

So much so that it was to him she turned when, a few weeks before her seventeenth birthday, she discovered that she was pregnant by Michael, her first and only proper boyfriend. Michael himself must not know, certainly not just before his exams. He was a sixth-former, too, brilliant and expected to get a State Scholarship to study medicine. Nothing must get in the way of his future. Dad would understand. Dad wouldn't blow his top and shout and scream at her. Dad would help.

William was shattered, but he couldn't think of letting Vicky down. There was a lot of talk about reforming the law against abortion, but it would be years before anything was done about it. He knew better than to believe old wives' tales about hot baths and plenty of gin, and it was out of the question for his beloved Vicky to fall into the hands of some ghastly creature wielding a metal coat hanger in a sordid room on a back street. William had friends in the brigade, and one of them put him in touch with another friend who knew of a distinguished surgeon on Wimpole Street. His views were liberal and humane, and he could occasionally be persuaded to put his career in jeopardy by helping a girl in distress; but he was expensive.

William did not have the necessary five hundred pounds, and since he and Audrey had a joint bank account, he could not arrange a loan without involving her. It must have been when he realized this that he began to lose his mind, because any sane building society branch manager knew very well that the society's procedures incorporated elaborate safeguards which insured that if he were to advance five hundred pounds to a fictitious mortgage applicant he would be found out within a matter of days. Those safeguards further made it certain that if, as William Parsons did, he took the money in cash during the course of a working day, he was asking for trouble within hours.

In William's case a Miss Julie Withers suspected that her till was short at two-twenty, checked it again, and turned to her colleague Beverly Connolly who was really Mrs. Drew but preferred to use her maiden name at work. Beverly said no, Julie surely knew she wouldn't raid her till for fivers without saying so, and well, blow me down, mine's short, too. The assistant manager Mr. Wilson was thereupon consulted. Mr. Wilson was a bit on the officious side, but quick on the uptake, and he saw at once that this was a matter for Mr. Parsons. So at two thirty-five he rushed, without knocking, into the manager's office to find its occupant putting a rubber band round a stack of five-pound notes.

There were any number of ways in which William Parsons could have talked himself out of what was admittedly an unorthodox situation, but he panicked, thrust the money into his pocket, and bolted out of the room and the building. At two forty-two he was apprehended by PC Godfrey Hislop, and by three-thirty he had been formally charged. So frenzied was his behavior that he was kept in custody, and further remanded in custody by the magistrates who committed him for trial.

When William Parsons eventually came before Mr. Justice Thumper, he was no longer in a state of agitation, but was lost in the dark night of the soul. For Vicky, bereft of her father's help, had, on the basis of her pathetically elementary medical knowledge, tried to abort herself, been discovered in agony too late, and died in the hospital. His defense counsel persuaded William to plead not guilty, but after that he remained mute throughout the trial, while his barrister argued temporary insanity caused by anxiety about his daughter's health. It was a tricky line to take, because had it emerged in court that Parsons had taken the money to pay for an illegal operation things would have been all the worse for him.

Mr. Justice Thumper poured scorn on the temporary insanity idea, even though, under cross-examination, Mr. Wilson the assistant manager agreed that as an experienced official of the Reliable Building Society the accused must have known that his actions could only result in disaster for him. Here, the judge insisted in his summing-up to the jury, was a man in a position of trust and solemn financial responsibility who, they might well conclude, had betrayed that trust, and in a blatantly outrageous way.

It was only when the members of the jury had duly brought in their guilty verdict that Thumper really let himself go, in passing sentence following defense counsel's plea for mitigation on the grounds that his client's distress of mind had been immeasurably increased by the fact that his daughter had in fact died. That was unfortunate no doubt, His Lordship thundered, but justice must be done. His condemnation of the transgressions of the prisoner in the dock was exceptionally fiery and protracted even by his own exacting standards, and long before he had finished, counsel on both sides knew that the wretched, shambling man in the dock would be going down for a long time.

William Parsons heard the words through the mists of his misery, and dimly understood their import. It didn't matter to him. Nothing did, until the sanctimonious old fool went too far, by seeming to imply—he was sure he had—that darling Vicky's death was a judgment from Heaven. For almost the first time in the trial, he raised his head and looked directly at the judge. The fog of despair was dissipated, washed away by the bright hatred that was to give him back the will to live, and sustain him through the years of imprisonment.

The scoreboard read one set all, and five games to four in Nancy Wiesendonck's favor in the third. However, Trish had been coming up fast, it was her service game and she had dropped only one point in it. Forty–fifteen. It was after all only an exhibition match, but Nancy Wiesendonck looked as grim as any top-class player facing three game points and the likelihood of a long battle to come was entitled to.

The English girl took a deep breath which deeply moved Nigel Colveden, swung . . . and the ball shot off at a tangent. Her second serve was in, but so feeble that her opponent was able to smash it back almost contemptuously. Forty-thirty. The next point also went to the American, following another poor service and another strong return. Deuce, and then a double fault. Advantage Miss Wiesendonck, and Miss Thumper blundering about the court like a hopelessly outclassed beginner.

"She's ill," Mel Forby said to Thrudd Banner.

"She's lost," he replied a few seconds later, when slightly puzzled applause broke out and Trish Thumper trailed listlessly to the net to shake hands with the victor, in whose face satisfaction vied with concern.

There was nothing but concern in that of Sir Wilfred Thumper, and nothing but satisfaction in that of William Parsons as the two young women thanked the umpire and left the court together, one of them in obvious distress.

chapter 3

"LET'S SEE, when is it you're finally taking the plunge, Bob?"

Detective Sergeant Bob Ranger looked across the office to where his boss was sitting fiddling with his letter opener. Not that the Oracle ever seemed to use it for its proper purpose, very few documents reaching his desk were in envelopes anyway. It gave him something to play with, though, and a bit of exercise because he dropped it so often and had to bend down to retrieve it. "Saturday week, sir. You and Mrs. Delphick're coming, you accepted. And, um . . . you did approve my application for two weeks leave, a couple of months back."

No harm in reminding him of that crucial fact, putting it firmly on the table and dusting it off right away. Because the Oracle had that file in front of him, the one he'd brought back after going to see Sir Heavily the previous day and kept locked away since then. And he had that look about him, the look that said something new was in the wind. Typical, just as they were getting the backlog of paper work sorted out at last so that he'd be able to leave everything shipshape. Could even guess what the old devil was thinking—something along the lines of, here's an interesting bucket of worms that'll keep you occupied for a nice long time, my lad.

"There's no need to look so apprehensive. I remember perfectly well, and am painfully reconciling myself to the prospect of doing without your services while you and Anne are off sunning yourselves in wherever it is you're being so secretive about. Have no fear, my wife and I will report at Plummergen parish church in good time in our glad rags. I might be able to make myself useful when the vicar asks if anybody knows of any let or hindrance to the marriage. I could marshal the objectors into an orderly queue."

"Good of you, sir." Whatever it was, couldn't be worrying him all that much if the Oracle was acting so pleased with himself.

"Think nothing of it." Delphick waved his hand in airy acknowledgment and the letter opener flew from it and clattered to the floor. He hauled himself out of his chair and went to fetch it. "I'm looking forward to visiting Plummergen again. The Ideal Spot To Tie The Knot. I hope you heard me pronounce the capital letters. D'you know I actually saw that on a sign once, outside a wedding chapel in Nevada? But that's by the way. Thing is, I've a little job for you, arising out of the contents of this slim file." Being still on his feet, Delphick took it over to his assistant.

"You will find inside five threatening letters, with their envelopes, received at irregular intervals over the past few months by Sir Wilfred Thumper, the judge well-known for his Old Testament attitudes and quotable *obiter dicta*. In the past couple of years he's acquired a second claim to fame as the father of Trish Thumper, the tennis player said by some to be in with an outside chance at Wimbledon this year. You'll also find a confidential note dictated by no less than the commissioner in person, following a little chat he had with the judge. Now all I require from you is the name of the joker doing the menacing. Simple enough to dredge up for a chap with your talents."

Ranger opened the file and stared at its meager contents for a moment before trusting himself to speak. Then he closed his eyes briefly as if in prayer, and only then raised his head again. "I wouldn't even know how to begin. Have a heart, sir."

"Come now, I do have a heart, the heart of a small boy. It's in a jar on my mantelpiece at home. So I'll take pity and guide you up the nursery slopes. As you see, the letters have been placed in a clear plastic envelope, presumably because some amateur—whether the judge or the commissioner I wouldn't like to say—having almost certainly put his own dabs all over them, then thought the author might have obligingly done the same. I doubt very much if he or she would have done anything so foolish, though they'll have to be checked, for form's sake. The envelopes have been handled by umpteen post office employees so they're obviously useless from that point of view. Or from any other, very likely. They look as if they came from Woolworths, they're correctly addressed but in childish block capitals, and all seem to have been posted in Central London."

"But good grief, sir, why bother, anyway? Hate mail's an occupational hazard for judges. And people like us. Remember that bloke two or three years ago, used to write to you in green ink once a week as regular as clockwork, threatening I don't know what?"

Delphick smiled reminiscently. "Yes indeed. The juicy bits underlined in red. And he became so frustrated at getting no reaction that in the end he enclosed a stamped, addressed envelope for my reply. Turned out to be the father of the chap who twisted his ankle coming downstairs with a pillowcase full of costly trinkets and waltzed into my welcoming arms."

"Yes, well, I mean to say, sir. You used to chuck his letters in the wastepaper basket. Why doesn't this judge do the same?"

"Great minds think alike. I made that very suggestion to the assistant commissioner, but then he explained the background and I had to agree that circumstances alter cases. Read the commissioner's note, Bob. Mr. Justice Thumper has been handing out maximum sentences and blistering remarks for years, on circuit as well as at the Bailey. So, not surprisingly, his mailbag has yielded many a colorful warning that vengeance is nigh. He is a crusty old bigot, but not easily intimidated. He's therefore in the habit of giving no more than a cursory glance at such missives before burning them. The commissioner notes that Thumper reckons he dealt with two, maybe three earlier letters from this fellow—I think it's a man—in that way. They were rambling and unspecific, what you might call run-of-the-mill to an old hand like His Lordship, but the next one upset him, because in it the author came to the point and threatened his daughter Patricia, alias Trish. And as you'll see, he repeated the threat in the following four, the last three of which were received during the last ten or twelve days."

"What a louse! Does the poor kid know?"

"No. Thumper's kept it from her and her mother. And since he's presumably far from being a ray of sunshine at the best of times, they might not have noticed that he has a bad and understandable case of the jitters. Anyway, our masters have ordained that a protective eye is to be kept on Miss Thumper until we run the mystery man to earth."

Delphick looked at his watch. "And that reminds me that I must be off to do something about that," he added, and made for the door, where he paused. "Get the fingerprint tests out of the way quickly. Immerse yourself in the Olympian thoughts of the commissioner. We're almost certainly looking for somebody Thumper sent down for a long stretch, and who got out late last year. Woo the computers, Bob. Let's see what sort of a short list of candidates the beastly machines can draw up." Then he was gone.

It wasn't much, but enough to enable Ranger temporarily to thrust thoughts of invitation lists, wedding presents, and the cost of furniture and fitted carpets to the back of his mind and address himself to the file; but before he had begun to read the note dictated by the commissioner, the door was opened again and Delphick's head appeared round it.

"I forgot to swear you to silence," he said sternly. "The press must on no account get wind of this affair. Quite apart from all the other good reasons, it would muck up my plan to exploit the interesting Plummergen connection. Oh yes, there is one. You'll get to it in a minute."

"Yes, sir, of course. The two things go together. Until we can identify and deal with the originator of the threats, we must do everything within reason to ensure that Miss Thumper comes to no harm. Now as to the first, I've already given instructions for a list to be drawn up, of the names of people sentenced to significant stretches by her father and who were released about the end of last year. No guarantee that the man we're looking for is among them, but it's an obvious possibility and we've got to start somewhere. I've no idea how many names we'll come up with, but even if there are comparatively few, it'll be a time-consuming job to find out their current whereabouts and check up on them."

"Fair enough. Ask for whatever help you need on that. What's to be done about the girl?"

"I have a suggestion to make there, sir. I've made discreet

inquiries about Trish Thumper's forthcoming public appearances, before Wimbledon itself, I mean, and she's due only to play at Hastings, in about ten days' time. She lost an exhibition match at Hurlingham yesterday, incidentally. Bit of a last-minute upset, according to the paper this morning. In the normal way she travels a lot, of course, taking part in various tournaments all over the place, but home is with her parents here in London so I suppose that's where she plans to base herself for the time being. In the circumstances I think she'd be better off elsewhere, because the man we're after knows the Thumper address."

Sir Hubert frowned. "Don't altogether follow you there. Why not simply put a uniformed man outside the front door? That'd stop his nonsense."

"Not necessarily, I'm afraid, sir. She's got to go to and fro to practice every day at the Queen's Club or wherever she trains. Fellow might still be able to make a nuisance of himself and upset her badly. And there's another thing. Even if he manages to keep his worries to himself, her father must be in a very twitchy state. It could make for an uneasy atmosphere and I understand these sports stars are easily put off their stroke."

"Tender plants, eh? Fair enough in the case of a young woman, I s'pose. It's these frightful long-haired football players hugging and kissing each other in public that get my goat. Well, I see your point, Delphick. What's the alternative?"

"I can think of one that has its attractions, sir. Hastings isn't all that far from Plummergen by car, and Sir George Colveden lives just outside Plummergen."

"So what?"

"Well, sir, now that we know he and Thumper are lifelong cronies, it occurs to me that the Colvedens would probably be happy enough to put Miss Thumper up for a while at Rytham Hall, incognito. They're kindly, hospitable people, and she must know them well and feel at home with them. Sir Wilfred would be reassured by the idea that she was under their protection, and without drawing attention to the fact we could lay on a discreet background presence. Even ferry her back and forth to Hastings —where she could presumably do her training—in an unmarked car."

The assistant commissioner pondered almost audibly, and then directed a glare of deep suspicion at his subordinate. "Well?" he inquired.

"Sir?"

"Come off it, Oracle. Why have you so ostentatiously failed to mention that Miss Emily Seeton also lives in Plummergen? And that if there is any conceivable—or indeed *inconceivable*—way in which she can become inextricably involved in this affair, then involved she will most assuredly become?"

"Actually, Miss Seeton would be part of the discreet background presence I envisage, sir. She is on a retainer from us, after all." Delphick raised his eyes heavenward. "And you must admit that somebody up there seems to like her."

Everleigh glanced up, too. "Don't be absurd, the commissioner's never even met her."

"I'd forgotten for the moment that his office is directly above yours, sir. Actually, I was referring to the Almighty."

"So was I, Chief Superintendent. Let us not forget who we both work for." Delighted at having for once defeated Delphick in a battle of wits, Sir Hubert decided to quit while he was ahead. "Very well. On the whole it doesn't sound a bad idea, provided it can be set up without too much trouble and the young lady herself approves. You'd better get in touch with both Colveden and Thumper and try it out on them. Thumper's been given your name as the person to contact in all this business, by the way, so he won't be surprised to hear from you. And you know Colveden already. Keep me posted."

chapter 4

"SHE'S BACK, Bunny," Miss Erica Nuttel announced grimly, allowing the net curtain to drop back into place.

"Who ith, aagh?" Mrs. Norah Blaine had been trying to persuade a length of embroidery silk through the eye of a needle, a fiddly job for which she needed to stick her tongue out, and omitted to reel it in before responding to her friend, who turned and surveyed her.

"Why are you squawking like that?"

"You made me bite my tongue and my eyes water, Eric."

"I did no such thing. If you weren't so vain you'd wear your glasses, and then you wouldn't keep sticking it out in the first place."

Having partly recovered her composure and wiped her eyes with the back of her hand, Mrs. Blaine managed a timid smile. "I'll try to remember, in future. Promise. Who's back?"

"The frightful journalist person who wrote all those beastly things about the village in the *Daily Negative* after That Woman held up the post office."

This was a little too much even for the staunchly loyal Bunny. "Well, actually, it did turn out that we formed a misleading—"

"Nonsense! The police and the press connived to hush up the true facts. They're always doing it. You can't even rely on the *Daily Telegraph* these days. She's left her car outside the George and Dragon. Probably too drunk to trust herself to drive." Miss Nuttel peered out of the window again, and Mrs. Blaine went over and joined her. "There you are. Distinctly unsteady on her feet, as you can see. Well no, you probably can't, without your glasses, but she is, take my word for it. And you don't need me to tell you where she's heading for. Sweetbriars."

Miss Nuttel pronounced the name of Miss Seeton's cottage in such a way that, hearing it, a stranger could well be prompted to form a mental picture of the sinister lair of an evil witch. In fact the modest dwelling Miss Seeton had, while still teaching art in London, inherited from her godmother was aptly named, and Plummergen itself a pleasant Kentish village, if hardly the sort of which picture postcards are made.

"Really? I wonder why she should be going to see Miss Seeton?"

"Because the pair of them are partners in crime, of course. And I should imagine that whatever business they have to discuss isn't the kind that can be done over the telephone. Just think of some of the things that have happened since That Woman moved here! Arson, forgery, witchcraft, murder, jewel thefts. We've personally seen her savagely assault an innocent bird watcher. And don't forget she put a bomb in that unfortunate man's car. She's a menace to society."

"Yes, but Eric, according to the newspapers, it was his own bomb that he'd planted in her house, trying to kill her. And all the other times, she was *helping* the police, they say. Constable Potter won't hear a word against her."

Miss Nuttel withered her with a smile. "That just proves

my point. Potter is clearly under instructions to take that line. For the very good reason that she has powerful protectors at Scotland Yard, high-ranking Freemasons, I expect. Look how they covered up for Jack the Ripper. Potter may well be one himself."

"Potter a Freemason?"

"Appearances can be deceptive, Bunny. I know he looks and behaves like a rustic simpleton, but I sense a certain low, animal cunning about that man. Anyway, it's my belief that this journalist creature and the Seeton woman are able to lead their charmed lives because they know certain things that various senior policemen cannot afford to have revealed. So the so-called authorities pay the price for their silence."

Mrs. Blaine opened her myopic eyes wide. "Blackmail, Eric?" she breathed.

Miss Nuttel nodded curtly and hitched up the waistband of her slacks. "And I mean to get to the bottom of it," she said, moving toward the door. "You stay here, Bunny. I intend to shadow this corrupt Forby person."

Mrs. Blaine gazed at her in admiration. "Oh, Eric, you're so decisive! But do be careful, won't you?"

Mel Forby wasn't in the least drunk, but she had enjoyed a single glass of wine in the bar with one of the George and Dragon's rare roast beef sandwiches, about the only good thing to be had there. It was pleasant to be back in Plummergen and strolling down its single street, imaginatively called The Street. It would have been even better had Thrudd Banner been at her side, but he was in Germany, having managed to secure an exclusive interview with Chancellor Willy Brandt. Mel was sublimely uninterested in international politics and couldn't imagine why Thrudd had ever gone in for that kind of journalism in the first place, before deciding to double up as a photographer, too.

Thrudd was all right, though. It was fun the way they joshed each other all the time. Good, clean fun. Kind of a shame it was always such good, *clean* fun, but—now that's quite enough of that, Forby. Impure thoughts are out of order when you're on your way to talk to Miss Emily D. Seeton. Wonder what the D stands for. Not Delilah, that's for sure. Dorothy? Daphne? Something quiet and respectable, anyway.

And here we are at Sweetbriars. Tap on the door. No answer. Tap again, still no answer. Out to lunch? Try door, unlocked, peek inside. "Yoohoo! Anybody home?"

Strange. No reply, but a distinct sound of, what, something between a grunt and a moan, oh for heaven's sake, the poor old thing isn't in trouble, is she? Pound up the stairs, open bedroom door, and—gee, what a relief! Just a case of whatchamacallit, *déjà vu*. Even the old-fashioned stockings and bloomers looked familiar, but it was the way Miss S. was sitting on the floor, her lower legs splayed out on either side of her in a peculiar way and her feet somehow turned back out of sight behind her that really took a girl back to her first visit to this bedroom.

"Cow-Face!" Mel yelled delightedly, and then waited, grinning until Miss Seeton uttered a single word, loudly and explosively, because she was expelling a deep abdominal breath at the same time.

"*Frog!* Oh dear, I didn't mean to shout. Not Cow-Face, actually. I was practicing the Frog Posture. Cow-Face is like this," Miss Seeton added in a more subdued tone, flinging one arm up and over her shoulder and the other sideways behind her back, joining her hands there without apparent effort. "But how nice that you remembered the name." She disengaged her arms and smiled. "Good afternoon, er, Mel." Oh dear, one really was too set in one's ways to find it at all easy to use first names, but dear Miss Forby was so insistent that it would be impolite not to . . .

"Trust me to get it wrong. Sorry to come busting in on you like that. It sounded as if you might be in some sort of trouble, but I should have known better. The yoga's going well, then?"

"Reasonably well, thank you. Many of the Group B postures will, I fear, always be beyond me. They should not be attempted by elderly persons who come late in life to hatha yoga, and certainly not while alone. Balancing Tortoise, Yogin's Staff, and so forth."

"Wow, they sound pretty wild. And here was I congratulating myself on remembering Cow-Face. Mind you, I could hardly forget it, I thought you were being rude to me that other time." Miss Seeton having untangled her arms and legs, Mel stretched out her hand, helped her to her feet, and then into her dressing gown. "Actually, it was a pretty fair description of the way I looked in those days," she added, blushing a little at recalling the extravagant makeup she had been in the habit of affecting before coming under Miss Seeton's civilizing influence.

"Such nonsense! Now, why don't you go downstairs and put the kettle on? While I make myself look a little more respectable. Then we'll have a nice chat. Dear dear, I should have emptied that this morning." Miss Seeton reached for the carafe of drinking water from her bedside table. "Waste not want not," she said, crossing to the open window. "During this very dry spell we're being asked to economize by not watering our gardens with hose-pipes." With her head still turned toward Mel, she stretched out her arm and upended the carafe. The simple action was followed immediately by the sound of a stifled scream from outside, and Miss Seeton leaned in consternation out the window.

"Oh, my goodness, I am so very sorry, Miss Nuttel!" she cried. "How dreadfully thoughtless of me! Do please allow me to offer you a dry towel—Miss Nuttel, do come back . . ." She stood leaning out the window for another few seconds before turning back with a look of puzzled concern to Mel, who had temporarily collapsed into a fit of giggling. "She's, well . . . running away, Mel. Her hair quite drenched. How *awful*. What must she think of me?"

Mel wiped her eyes. "You soused Erica Nuttel? Terrific! Don't worry, we already know what the Nuts think of you, Miss S. I'll bet you anything you like she spotted me on my way here. Followed me and hung about outside to snoop. Poetic justice, I call it."

A towel wound round her head in the shape of a turban, and somewhat fortified by the cup of strong, sweet tea that Norah Blaine had distractedly made for her, Miss Nuttel sat and brooded.

"Microphones," she said eventually.

"Microphones?"

"Of course. That house must be wired for sound. Or be surrounded by one of those, what do you call them, infrared beams. The Seeton woman could not possibly have known I was outside the window unless some kind of silent alarm had alerted her. The two of them were having a violent argument, you see."

"What about?"

"How on earth should I know? I arrived just as they were screaming vulgar insults at each other—cow, frog, and so on. Then I must have triggered off the alarm, because all at once they lowered their voices, and then, a second later . . ."

"How *awful* for you, Eric! Are you quite sure you

oughtn't to have a hot bath? You might catch a chill otherwise."

"Do be quiet and let me think. I have no intention of allowing myself to be outmaneuvered by those women. They are clearly plotting some new outrage, and as public-spirited citizens we must do whatever we can to frustrate them."

Chief Superintendent Delphick had a lot to think about on the way back to Scotland Yard from the stately Kensington house in which Sir Wilfred Thumper resided with his wife Lavinia (who was one of the Bockleton family of Shropshire, and therefore possessed of a large independent fortune) and their daughter Patricia. Following his conversation with the assistant commissioner he had been on the point of telephoning to make an appointment with the judge, only to be beaten to it. Mr. Justice Thumper had not bothered with preliminary courtesies. "Is that Delphick? Wilfred Thumper. I want to see you immediately. I shall expect you at my house in half an hour."

Delphick was a man blessed with an equable temperament who seldom allowed himself to be put out, but he had nevertheless been in an extremely frosty mood by the time he had arrived at the house. One look at the man who had summoned him was enough to make him forget that he was offended; quite apart from the fact that the judge's opening words were "Thank God you're here." Thumper was clearly a man near the end of his tether, and the letter he had received by the second post that morning and thrust into Delphick's hands as soon as they were closeted in his study made it unnecessary to speculate about the reasons.

The postmark on the cheap brown envelope indicated that it had been mailed in London, SW6, in time to catch the last collection the previous evening. It and the single sheet of lined paper it contained resembled the ones now under scrutiny by the forensic experts, but the message was the bleakest yet, and short enough for Delphick to have memorized it:

> THUMPER YOU BASTARD. ENJOY WATCHING HER LOSE? THE LOOK ON YOUR FACE WAS A TREAT AND I ONLY GAVE HER GUTS-ACHE THIS TIME. WAIT TILL I GET GOING.

Trish Thumper had, it seemed, insisted after the match that her sudden indisposition must have been due to something she had eaten, that it was rotten luck it had hit her at such a crucial moment, but that it was just a spot of tummy trouble and that she'd be as right as rain after a good night's sleep. She had indeed on getting up that morning claimed that she felt much better, if still a bit queasy, and was resting in her room.

After reading the letter her father had wanted to pack her off at once to the London Clinic for medical tests, but Trish was a strong-minded young woman who firmly refused, and of course Thumper couldn't explain why he was so agitated, so there the matter rested for the moment. Well, Delphick thought to himself, at least it had made the old curmudgeon more than receptive to his idea that she should if possible be consigned to the care of the Colvedens at Rytham Hall for the time being, and Thumper had agreed with almost pathetic eagerness to try to arrange it through his old friend Sir George.

Meantime, it looked as if they'd have to pull all the stops out and hurry to identify this joker. Manifestly, he'd been present at the exhibition match at the Hurlingham Club the previous afternoon, witnessed the debacle, and posted his letter in the vicinity immediately afterwards. What's more, he claimed to have been responsible for Trish's unexpected and disastrous loss of form in the crucial game.

Now that wasn't necessarily so: he might have had nothing to do with it. Anybody could suddenly get a bad case of the collywobbles while involved in strenuous physical activity on a warm summer afternoon. The mystery man might simply have noticed that after playing very well Trish suddenly found herself in trouble, twigged what was happening, and cleverly seen it as a chance to put additional heat on Thumper by claiming the credit for it, as it were. On the other hand, he might genuinely have contrived somehow to slip the girl some sort of mickey.

Whatever the true explanation, it seemed pretty clear that they were up against somebody more formidable than it had been tempting to suppose. Somebody who was very strongly motivated indeed, and who knew a bit about how to pile on the pressure.

Lady Colveden put down her trowel and sat back on her heels, kneeling comfortably on the old bit of carpet she used when gardening. Whenever her husband drifted alongside like that and started aimlessly whistling and jingling the keys in his pocket, she knew there was something on his mind. "What is it, George? Have you broken a plate or something?"

"Plate? What plate? Why on earth should you suddenly accuse me of breaking a plate? Anybody would think I make a habit of smashing crockery. Why, I haven't broken anything since—"

"The day before yesterday. Very well, I apologize. All the same, you look as if you've got a guilty conscience."

Meg Colveden looked up affectionately at the elderly gentleman in tweeds who was shuffling about beside her. He might be—indeed undoubtedly was—not only a retired major general and holder of a DSO, but also a baronet, a knight commander of the Order of the Bath, and a justice of the peace: he still looked slightly ashamed of himself and she knew from experience that he was about to tell her a fib.

"Not at all, m'dear, not at all. Just had young Thumper on the phone, as a matter of fact. Chatted about this and that, you know. Always good to hear from him."

"Considering the three of them were here only last week, you couldn't have had all that much news to catch up on. I wonder what he'd say if he knew you call him 'young Thumper'? He can't be far off sixty, after all. And he hasn't improved with age, in my purely personal opinion."

"Four years younger than I am, Meg. Big difference when you're boys. Lot of people don't care for him, I know. Bit of a tartar in court, they say, but I found him a good enough lad, if a bit slow on the uptake. Had to whack him a few times to get him to grasp that the jam has to be spread right up to the edges of a piece of toast, but after that no trouble at all. And for some odd reason he still seems to look up to me, you know. Can't think why, but there you are."

"Look up to you! He hero-worships you, George. If I didn't know you better, I might . . . well, anyway, what did he want?"

"Want? Oh, nothing in particular. Got some tickets for that highbrow opera place over in Sussex. Wanted to know if we'd care to go."

"Glyndebourne? How splendid! We'd love to go, George."

"Would we? Oh. I may have rather put him off, but I've promised to ring him back, anyway." Sir George shuffled his feet and cleared his throat. "Fact is, I was wondering how you'd feel about inviting Patricia to stay here for a few days.'' Once he had finally got it out, he felt much better.

''Why?''

''Why not? Charmin' girl, I thought when they all came to tea. And if I'm not much mistaken, Nigel took a definite shine to her.''

Lady Colveden stood up and brushed herself down. ''Dear George, Nigel takes a definite shine to any and every presentable young woman who comes within half a mile of him. And this is the first time you've shown any inclination to play matchmaker. Now Patricia is a nice enough girl if a bit hearty, and I haven't the slightest objection to inviting her here if she'd like to come. But you'll have to do a bit better than those for reasons.''

''Ah. Hm. Yes, well, it seems she's a bit under the weather. Lot of strain, Wimbledon coming up, you know. Bit of country air might put the roses back in her cheeks, eh? And it's not all that far from here to Hastings, Thumper says. She's got to go in for some contest or other at Hastings, it seems. And come to think of it, neither is this Glyndebourne place you seem so keen on, and Nigel could always—''

''George, you are waffling. Stop it. You and Wilfred Thumper are clearly up to something, but if you're not disposed to tell me, I shall work it out for myself. Now go and tell him we shall be happy to welcome Patricia here for as long as she'd like to stay, and yes, we would most certainly love to go to Glyndebourne. I expect I shall need a new dress to go in, by the way.''

chapter 5

William Parsons drove the ambulance into the garage at the small Cranhurst Ambulance Station, performed his going-off-duty checks, and locked up. Then he changed out of his uniform in the cramped little locker room and glanced at his watch before signing himself out on the duty time sheet. Thursday evening, just after six and he wasn't due on again until Monday morning.

Cranhurst was a market town, too small to have a proper emergency ambulance service manned round the clock. That part of Sussex was served in that respect from East Grinstead; and Parsons and the other permanent driver based at Cranhurst mostly spent their days ferrying old people between hospitals, day-care centers, and nursing homes, or taking patients to and from the hospital for routine therapy. Sometimes a nurse went along, but usually the drivers worked alone, which suited Parsons very well. He liked the old folk, even the cranky ones, remembered the names and complaints of his regulars, and listened patiently when they rambled on.

He knew he had been lucky, to get the job six months ago when he'd been released. It wasn't easy for ex-cons to find secure, respectable work, even educated ones whose offences had not involved violence. Having taken the trouble to look into his background, the probation officer had been sympathetic and done well by him. Not that it had been all that difficult to fix him up in the Sussex County Ambulance Service, because apart from the fact that he'd done time, he was well qualified.

There couldn't be all that many applicants for ambulance driver posts who'd passed the St. John's Ambulance Brigade's advanced first-aid examinations with distinction and indeed served as a volunteer instructor. If only Audrey hadn't divorced him, things might have turned out very differently. But then if he hadn't been sent to prison, she probably wouldn't have. And he wouldn't have met and shared a cell for a long time with Norman Proctor, who if he knew him would have arrived at the Goat and Compasses bang on opening time, and whose help was essential if his long-cherished plan was to succeed.

"Lost twelve'n' 'alf minutes o' valuable drinkin' time, you 'ave, mate," Norm said. "Drag up a bollard an' meet 'Arvey. 'Arve, this is Bill."

"Lovely," said Harvey, extending a limp hand which Parsons shook as briefly as possible. Norm had said he'd be bringing a friend along, but not that the person in question would be wearing mascara and an earring, have dyed blond hair with more than a hint of pink in it, or be dressed in a frilled shirt open almost to the waist and tight velvet trousers flared at the ankles.

"Get the man a beer, 'Arve," Norm commanded, and Harvey rose at once and made for the bar, bestowing a melting smile and flutter of the eyelashes on Parsons as he edged sinuously past him. "Cheer up, Bill," Norm went on when Harvey was out of earshot. "I know 'e looks a right nelly, but 'e knows 'is stuff, does 'Arvey. I met 'is

Mum once. Quite a surprise, it was." He winked at Parsons. "If I'm any judge, she must've bin a right little goer in 'er day."

"I hope you haven't told him any of my business, Norm."

"Nah. No need yet awhile. Wait 'n see, once you get to know 'im you'll trust 'im. An' you never know, if what I over'eard at that posh tennis club's kosher, a fancy-lookin' poofter like young 'Arvey might come in 'andy later on. Ah, there you are, took your time, din't yer?"

Harvey set a brimming pint glass of beer down delicately before Parsons and then insinuated himself back into his own chair and addressed him earnestly. "Now, dear, I'm sure Norman's been saying the most awful things about me. He's as common as dirt, you know, but we couldn't do without each other businesswise. And I'm sure you and I are going to get on just deliciously. It's so exciting to know you're going to drive for us in this part of the world. The creature we had in the Midlands was quite sweet in his way, but utterly *disastrous* behind the wheel."

"Like I said, Bill, when we 'ad our little chat the other day at the tennis. 'Arve 'n me, we bin sussin' out churches." An expression of sorrowful gravity swept over Norm's pale but lively features, and he wagged his head slowly from side to side. "It's a shockin' thing, but there's a lot more light-fingered people about than what there was, me ol' mate. Not like the old days when a feller could reckon on nippin' inside an 'ouse o' God any ol' time for a quick shufti an' away with a nice little candlestick or whatever. Nah, praggly all the ones in towns are locked up all the time now, 'cept for Sunday services. Night *an'* day. Wossmore, they stash their good stuff away in the bank. Now I ask you, what sorter way's that to praise the 'Oliest in the 'Eight? An' things are startin' to go the same way even in the country. So 'Arve'n me, we gotter get our skates on, see?''

''What Norman's trying to explain in his crude, untutored way, dear, is that the race is to the swift. There's still a deal of nice silverware just *lurking* in unlocked churches in little places off the beaten track, and sweet unwordly vicars and churchwardens simply *asking* to be relieved of it, you see. But nasty, suspicious insurance companies are beginning to badger them to lock up at night and install security systems, so we must make hay while the sun still shines. Poor, ignorant Norman here doesn't know a chalice from a chafing dish, or what's fenceable from what would bring the plods down on us like a ton of bricks, so that's where I come in.''

''Bin to Oxford College, 'e 'as,'' Norm said with pride. ''Reads books an' that. An' where *you* come in, sunshine, is as night duty driver an' lookout. We sussed out three beauties not a million miles from 'ere as can only be done after dark, see? All on the same night, no messin'. An' if you'll 'elp us out an' no questions asked, well, there shouldn't be no problem about that little favor *you* want doin'.''

Chief Inspector Chris Brinton of the Ashford Division of the Kent County Constabulary was having a bit of a cuddle on the sofa with Mrs. Brinton, who was ten years his junior, when the telephone rang. It was his birthday, after all. They'd had a bottle of wine with their evening meal, and one thing had led to another. It made a nice change for Mrs. Brinton to have a warm-up *before* they went up to bed, and she pulled a face as she popped her right breast back into the bra cup from which her husband had extricated it, and began to button up her blouse. Then, seeing Chris shake his head at her fiercely as he picked up the receiver, she unbuttoned it again. What the heck. If a girl couldn't go a bit mad in her own lounge, where could she?

"Brinton."

"Well, don't sound so gloomy about it, Chris. We each have our cross to bear. It's me, Delphick. Sorry to bother you at home."

"Oh. Hello, Oracle," Brinton said, averting his eyes from the distracting spectacle of his wife. For crying out loud, what he'd meant was that it'd be nice if she'd just stay like that on the sofa looking a bit pink and impatient, not stand up and sashay about in front of him languorously peeling off her blouse. "Do anything for you?"

Alone in his office at Scotland Yard, Delphick was puzzled by his old friend's unwontedly terse manner. "Look, if this is an inconvenient moment, say so."

"No, go . . . go ahead," Brinton said huskily. Mrs. Brinton had dropped her blouse to the carpet, and her arms were now snaking round her back to unfasten the bra. He closed his eyes, cleared his throat thunderously, and tried to concentrate on the quiet voice at his ear. "Oh. Really? Yeah. What? No, nothing special. Usual run of trouble. Some joker or jokers going the rounds lifting stuff from churches. Nuisance, but hardly a crime wave." He opened one eye and then closed it again hurriedly. Oh Gawd. The bra was draped over the arm of the sofa, the skirt was on the floor beside the discarded blouse, and Mrs. Brinton was removing her stockings, the glistening tip of her tongue moistening her lips as she did so.

"Yeah. Okay, thanks for telling me. I'll have a word with old Colveden in the morning and, nngyer . . . oooerhnngmf!"

The thunderous clattering noise the earpiece suddenly emitted was positively painful, and Delphic hastily moved the receiver an inch or so back. "Chris! Are you all right?

Chris?'' He listened again, hard. Brinton had obviously dropped the phone, but why? Silence at first . . . or was it? Was that the distant sound of a scuffle? Panting? Heavy breathing? Hoarse whispering? A woman's voice? A distinctly throaty giggle . . . oh, good grief! Smiling faintly, Delphick gently replaced the receiver in its cradle. Who'd ever have thought it of old Chris? And at eight forty-five in the evening.

After a moment's reflection, he picked up the phone again and dialed another Kent number. Whatever Miss Emily D. Seeton might be doing at that hour, she certainly wouldn't be indulging in nooky.

''Hello, Miss Seeton? Good evening. Delphick here, Scotland Yard. I thought I'd just ring to find out how you are and have a bit of a chat. I do hope I haven't chosen an inconvenient moment?''

''Mr. Delphick! Not at all, I was just amusing myself before cocoa time by making a few sketches . . . what a delightful surprise, and to think that we were talking about you just this afternoon, soon after I emptied the water jug on Miss Nuttel's head. I had been explaining the difference between Cow-Face and Frog to her, you see, and then happened to notice—''

''Excuse me, *what* exactly had you been explaining to Miss Nuttel?''

''No, not to Miss Nuttel, to Miss Forby. She remembered Cow-Face from the first time we met, but there are of course at least eighty-four fairly well-known yoga postures . . . ''

''Ah, yoga! Now I'm with you. At least, I think so. It wasn't Miss Nuttel you've been discussing me with, then? I must admit I'm rather relieved.''

''Oh dear me, no. I'm afraid she and Mrs. Blaine do seem to avoid me rather. Which is why I was so surprised at what happened. I was practicing the Frog posture, and Miss Forby mistook it for Cow-Face, and then I happened to notice that last night's drinking water was still there on the bedside table, so I emptied it out of the window on to the herbaceous border as usual, never dreaming that Miss Nuttel was outside. So as to economize, that is. During the dry spell."

Delphick found himself floundering, by no means for the first time when in converstion with Miss Seeton, and, never a man to mix his metaphors, decided to let the unspeakable Erica Nuttel sink or swim, and himself cling to the only life belt that seemed to be floating in his vicinity.

"You must have enjoyed seeing Mel Forby again. Did she drop in for any particular reason, or was she just passing through?"

"Well, Mr. Delphick, if you weren't a friend of hers, too, I'd hesitate to mention this, but I rather fancy that Mr. Banner might be the problem. Actually, she talked about Sir Wilfred Thumper a lot of the time. The judge, you know. It's my belief she's very fond of him, but he doesn't seem to have shown the same sort of interest in her so far."

Delphick screwed up his eyes, counted to five, and only then replied.

"Come now, Miss Seeton, I've known you too long to say the obvious thing. You aren't really implying that Mel Forby's in love with Wilfred Thumper, are you? You mean Thrudd Banner."

"With Sir Wilfred? Good gracious, no, of course not. Though Miss Forby—and Mr. Banner, as well, I gathered from her—do seem to be deeply interested in Sir Wilfred. To have somehow or other got wind of some, well, guilty secret of his."

Delphick gripped the telephone more tightly. For heaven's sake, if that pair had somehow got on to the blackmail business, they might as well put out a general press release on the subject. With a considerable effort of will he managed to keep his voice on an even keel. "Indeed? What sort of a guilty secret?"

"I have no idea, Mr. Delphick. Miss Forby hinted at a possible indiscretion in his youth, but I cannot imagine why she should suppose that I of all people might be able to throw any light on such a matter. It so happens that I have recently been introduced to the judge—he is an old friend of Sir George Colveden—but can scarcely claim his acquaintance on the strength of taking afternoon tea in his company. Tell me, Mr. Delphick, when did you last taste old-fashioned lemon curd? I did suggest to the vicar that it might have some significance for Sir Wilfred. Like the madeleine in Proust, you know—"

"I'm sorry to interrupt," Delphick said, then had to swallow because the thought of lemon curd had made his mouth water, "but oddly enough, I was going to ask if by any chance you were acquainted with the Thumper family. The daughter has in the last year or so become quite famous as a tennis player."

"Patricia, or Trish as she prefers to be called. Indeed yes, she was at Rytham Hall for tea with her parents. And she most generously arranged for Nigel to escort us, that is, the vicar and his sister and myself, to the Hurlingham Club at Fulham yesterday to watch her play. She was doing so well, too, when most unfortunately she seemed all at once to become unwell, and lost. It was cramp, Nigel said, but the poor boy was so disappointed for her that I expect it was the first thing that came into his head. To an American called Nancy Wiesendonck, I should have said. An uncommon name that made me wonder if there was perhaps a Wagner connection. Never mind, he's very happy now that Patricia has been invited to stay at Rytham Hall. Nigel, that is."

Delphick counted to five again; and then added three

more for good measure. "Er, Miss Seeton, did I hear you aright? You know that Trish Thumper is going to stay with the Colvedens? How?"

"How, Mr. Delphick? Why, it will be very little trouble for them, surely. There must be several spare bedrooms in such a huge house, and as the daughter of one of Sir George's oldest friends, I feel sure—"

"I mean how did you know?"

"Well, Nigel came and told us, this afternoon, as soon as he found out himself. It was rather touching. He was bursting with excitement. I do so hope that he won't suffer yet another disappointment. Perhaps this time the two young people might—"

"Miss Seeton, I'm sorry to interrupt you again, but you spoke of 'us'. Do you mean that Nigel Colveden told Mel Forby as well as yourself?"

"But of course, Mr. Delphick. Why ever shouldn't he?"

Delphick stifled an impulse to groan, and thought fast. It was bad enough that Mel Forby and Thrudd Banner seemed to be on to something or other about Thumper senior, though thank goodness it seemed to be connected with his past rather than the present. It would be interesting to know what it was, but that would have to wait.

That Mel Forby had now been handed on a plate the information that Trish Thumper was to be holed up at Rytham Hall was little short of disastrous. These were no run-of-the-mill hacks, but clever, persistently inquisitive people. It was going to be very tricky indeed to keep them on a leash. "Oh, um, no reason, I suppose," he said eventually. "It's just that my own impression was that the young lady wanted her visit to go unnoticed if possible. You know, avoid the attentions of the press while training for her big moment at Wimbledon."

"Oh dear."

"Never mind, I might have a word with Mel Forby myself. By the way, Miss Seeton, there's no need to mention to her that we've had this conversation. Well now, I'm looking forward to coming down to Plummergen myself and seeing you soon, at the wedding. Talk of the village, no doubt . . ."

Ten minutes later Delphick finally put the phone down and rubbed his eyes, trying to adjust himself to the new situation revealed by Miss Seeton. There was no point in worrying too much. Mel Forby and Thrudd Banner might, given the right kind of inducements, be persuaded to collaborate, at least for a time. As for Miss Seeton, well, with her head full of the local gossip about the forthcoming nuptials of Bob Ranger and Anne Wright the Plummergen doctor's daughter, she might not recall anything odd about their conversation. Not consciously, anyway. She was welcome to give her subconscious something to do. That was what Scotland Yard paid her for.

chapter 6

EVEN BEFORE Nigel Colveden dropped in at Sweetbriars for a cup of tea and a slice of Mrs. Bloomer's renowned fruit cake, Mel Forby had been in the process of deciding that there were, as usual, quite enough interesting vibes around Miss Seeton to make it worth her while to stop over in Plummergen for a day or two. The news Nigel conveyed so enthusiastically left her in no doubt where her place was. Later that afternoon she therefore booked herself into one of the better rooms at the George and Dragon, and made a couple of phone calls.

The first was to the editor of the *Daily Negative*, a man of whom most of her colleagues stood in awe. Having originally thought him formidable, Mel now knew exactly how to handle him. The editor, for his part, had learned to appreciate her and not to ask too many questions about her plans. It was enough for him to know that with a bit of luck Miss Emily D. Seeton, alias The Battling Brolly, would before long be back in action and the subject of an exclusive story by his star feature writer. Mel's expenses were guaranteed for as long as she cared to stay in Plummergen.

Her second call was brief: a matter of leaving a message for Thrudd Banner at his hotel in Bonn. Mel noted that the telephonist spoke very respectfully of Herr Banner; who hadn't returned her call until quite late in the evening, but it was worth the wait. It seemed that the German chancellor had been very forthcoming, that Thrudd expected to make a lot of money out of his article, and that he had wined and dined very well to celebrate the fact. In uninhibited mood he had said one or two things that made Mel go quite pink in the privacy of her room, and look forward more than ever to seeing him again. And this was to be in Plummergen, for Thrudd vowed to be in on whatever action seemed to be in prospect on his return to England in a day or two.

All in all, the following afternoon Amelita Forby looked upon life and found it good, even in the less than glamorous setting of Plummergen Village Hall, which had seen better days, and those a long time in the past.

The boy scouts no longer used it twice a week: their own hut had been completed three years earlier, and their gear transferred to it. They had however left behind them a slight but pervasive reminiscence of stale sweat, and their old plywood sign was still in place, mainly because it was mounted too high up on the dingy, brownish custard-colored plaster wall to be got at conveniently. In any case it was warped and tatty. 14TH PLUMMERGEN SCOUT TROOP, the curve of its faded, poorly executed lettering still proclaimed, forming a sort of halo round the top half of the fleur-de-lis badge with its BE PREPARED scroll underneath.

Mel Forby would have liked to ask somebody what had become of the other thirteen scout troops whose existence in or near the village was clearly implied. It seemed an extraordinary number for such a small place. Never during any of her numerous visits to Plummergen since Miss Seeton had taken possession of Sweetbriars had Mel knowingly come across so much as a lone boy scout, much less hordes of keen-as-mustard knot-tiers in khaki uniforms improvising bridges, lighting campfires, or helping old ladies across the street.

It occurred to her that the last-mentioned service would certainly be welcome in Plummergen, judging by the apparent age of some of the members of the Plummergen Women's Institute, now gathered for their quarterly business meeting under the chairmanship of Miss Molly Treeves. Among the senior citizens Mel recognized old Mrs. Wicks mumbling through her ill-fitting false teeth, and wondered whether she still told fortunes with the aid of playing cards. Others she remembered only vaguely, dodderingly functioning as a kind of Greek chorus in the background whenever events took a dramatic turn in Plummergen.

True, it would be hard to envisage Miss Treeves either needing or accepting assistance in crossing the road, or indeed in any other context. For she was in her full-figured, firmly corseted prime, resplendent that day in a flowered silk dress, her sash of office, and a quite dashing straw hat. And in fine fettle, too, nostrils flaring as she surveyed her audience of about three dozen women and then called the meeting to order.

"Good afternoon to you all. Before calling on the secretary and the treasurer to give us their reports, I want to say how happy I am to welcome a guest speaker, a very special guest speaker." Miss Treeves turned toward Mel, sitting alongside the institute's officers facing the rank and file, and bestowed a busy, rather menacing smile upon her. "As some of you know already, Mr. Windrush of the Easigro Nurseries who was to have addressed us today has, it seems, other more urgent business to attend to. But we are very far from being left in the lurch, for the famous Miss Amelita Forby of the *Daily Negative*, whose articles are read by millions, has most kindly and at very short notice agreed to allow us to take advantage of her . . . I mean of her being in Plummergen at this time, and we're all going to enjoy her after the business—''

''On a point of order, Madam Chairman!'' The interruption came from Erica Nuttel who had just bustled into the hall with Norah Blaine in her wake. Pausing dramatically near the door, she stood like a figure of doom, one arm extended and with her index finger pointing toward Mel. ''That woman—''

''You can't make a point of order. You haven't taken your seats, and in any case we haven't started yet.'' Miss Treeves's bosom heaved, and the light of joy in battle glinted in her eyes.

''Oh yes I can. I have consulted the copy of *Robert's Rules Of Order* they keep in the reference section at Brettenden Public Library and—''

''Be that as it may, Miss Nuttel. I *possess* a copy of the book in question—the latest edition—and my ruling is that you are *out* of order. Bursting in like that! You can jolly well sit down and wait until Any Other Business. Nowcallponsecretaryreport. Come along now, Mrs. Stillman.''

The generality of members sighed, and shifted in their seats with pleasure. Round one to Miss Treeves in what promised to be a more than usually satisfying encounter, and one they wouldn't want to end too soon. Though temporarily silenced, Miss Nuttel continued to point a quivering finger at Mel Forby for a second or two longer. Then she spotted two vacant chairs in the back row, towed Mrs. Blaine toward them, and sat down, realizing too late that the seat she had chosen was next to Mrs. Bloomer's and next but one to Miss Seeton's. Miss Seeton leaned forward and nodded a kindly greeting across her neighbor, while The Nuts affected not to notice her. Meantime Mrs. Stillman from the post office, who was able to be present in her capacity as honorary secretary because it was early closing day, rose as instructed to her feet, pushed her glasses back up to the bridge of her nose, and rustled her papers.

"Madam Chairman and members, it has been a busy and happy spring. Soon after our last meeting we celebrated the eighty-fifth birthday of one of our stalwarts, Mrs. Morgan, better known to most of us as dear Flo. On that occasion we all admired the way she blew out the eight big candles and five little ones on the splendid cake made by Mrs. Bloomer with materials kindly donated by Lady Colveden, and won't easily forget the way dear Flo regaled us over our chairman's homemade lemonade with the side-splitting story of how she mislaid her pension book a few years ago. On a more sober note, I must report that the Brettenden Town Clerk has acknowledged our representations about the improper nature of some of the private advertising postcards on display outside the tobacconists near the bus stop in the High Street there—"

"Disgusting! Will Pose in Traffic Warden Uniform indeed!"

Miss Treeves braced herself to deal with the irregular comment from the floor, but failed to identify the culprit and decided to let it pass as a permissible expression of outrage. Some of the cards—which she had made a special journey into Brettenden to inspect—indeed advertised photographic and massage services of a very suspect nature.

Others puzzled her rather. Dover with its cross-channel ferry services was not far away, but it seemed odd that so many ladies with Ashford, Canterbury, and even Brettenden telephone numbers could make a satisfactory living by giving French lessons privately. Especially when they stated their ages, which suggested that they must have qualified only quite recently as language instructors, yet went out of their way to stress that they were strict disciplinarians.

"—but regretted that there appeared to be no legal

grounds for intervention on his part. The competition for the best arrangement of fresh and dry foliage attracted a record number of entrants—'' Mrs. Stillman hastened on, for there had been ugly scenes after the judging—''and we take great pride in the fact that Miss Armitage's lovely display of white, cream, and yellow flowers, depicting the stages from milk to butter, has just walked away with the second prize at the regional WI show in Canterbury!''

Miss Armitage was a quiet soul who seldom offended anybody, and the news of her triumph provoked a ripple of applause, which Miss Treeves indulgently allowed to run its course.

''A well-attended meeting had as its high point an amusing talk by Mrs. Threlfall of the Embroidery Group, called 'In Stitches With Church Kneelers', and . . .''

I don't believe this, Mel reflected as Mrs. Stillman pressed on. They're all raving mad. And I'm crazy to have let La Treeves bulldoze me into facing them. Just because I walked slap-bang into her on the way out of Miss Seeton's garden gate. And then with my head full of the news about Trish Thumper, hardly paying attention while she was rabbiting on. About it being Miss S.'s turn to do the flowers, and some con man who'd promised what sounded like a real nail-biter of a talk on ''Handy Hints on Repotting'' and then let them down at the last minute. Hadn't seemed such a big deal at the time, and I was still feeling pretty good right up until The Nuts showed and the butch one in the trouser suit started hollering . . .

It was all right for Miss S., sitting there as quiet as a mouse beside Martha Bloomer with nothing to do but nurse the famous umbrella that went everywhere with her. The maniac Nut was obviously winding herself up to go on the rampage again, and this could turn out to be a bumpy ride for you, Forby . . .

"... and finally," said the honorary treasurer, who owned the drapery shop, had succeeded Mrs. Stillman at the lectern, and reported an encouraging credit balance of thirty-four pounds sixty-seven pence, "your committee have noted with pleasure that Anne Wright is to be married to Detective Sergeant Bob Ranger in the parish church next week, and I recommend that a telegram be sent on behalf of us all conveying our congratulations and best wishes to the happy couple. To be read out at the reception at the George and Dragon. The cost to be met out of institute funds."

"Will somebody second that?" Miss Treeves demanded, and Mrs. Potter shyly raised her hand. As the wife of PC Potter the village policeman, she felt it incumbent upon her to proclaim thus publicly her support for the law in all its manifestations, and perhaps particularly when it planned to get married in Plummergen parish church.

"I object!" Once more the ringing voice of Erica Nuttel was heard. "The police have a great deal to answer for in enabling your precious guest speaker and a certain person I don't care to name"—she whirled round to glare in the direction of Miss Seeton—"to bring notoriety and disgrace down upon this village, and I'm not a bit surprised that a certain other person has thought fit to second this outrageous proposal to squander our funds on—"

"All those in favor?" Even Miss Nuttel's words were lost in the splendid trumpeting sound the chairman produced, and hands were upraised all over the hall. Not having quite understood the motion, old Mrs. Wicks was rather slow off the mark, but joined in when her neighbor nudged her.

"Against?" Miss Treeves lowered the volume considerably, and smiled sweetly as she watched Erica Nuttel's arm shoot up and Norah Blaine's follow suit with less alacrity.

"Carried unanimously."

"*What?* This . . . this is a travesty of democracy! The national committee shall hear of this day's work—"

"Carried unanimously," Miss Treeves repeated. "I am advised by the honorary treasurer that the subscriptions of Miss Nuttel and Mrs. Blaine are three months in arrears. They are therefore ineligible to vote at this meeting. And come to think of it, you can't speak either, not even under Any Other Business. What on earth—?"

Even Mel, who naturally enough was keeping a watchful eye on The Nuts, wasn't quite sure about the precise sequence of events that accompanied the latter part of the chairman's ruling. It *looked* as if Miss Nuttel had started waving her arms about so violently that Martha Bloomer tilted her chair backwards in order to keep out of harm's way. But that unfortunately she overbalanced and fell to the floor, leaving a gap between Miss Seeton and the furious Nut, occupied only partially by Martha Bloomer's sturdy legs as they waved about.

Then, in leaning over her floundering housekeeper, umbrella still in hand, in an attempt to pull her back up to the vertical, it seemed that Miss Seeton had somehow managed to get the handle lodged in the waistband of Miss Nuttel's trousers. Which gave way audibly under the strain, slipped down her legs, and for a second or two afforded a number of fascinated members of the Women's Institute a glimpse of the serviceable pink underwear that lay beneath. No more than a glimpse, for with a strangled yelp of anguish the unhappy owner of the trousers yanked them up again and fled from the hall clutching at them and followed by Norah Blaine, who was—and it was the only possible word, Mel decided—*bleating*.

Having finally restored Mrs. Bloomer to an upright position and been reassured that she had sustained nothing worse than a loss of dignity, it was Miss Seeton who broke the stunned but appreciative silence which had descended over the meeting following the precipitate departure of The Nuts.

"Oh dear. I do most sincerely apologize, Madam Chairman. For my clumsiness, that is. I cannot imagine how—"

"Inasmuch as what we appear to have witnessed was an unprovoked assault on Mrs. Bloomer—are you unharmed after that nasty tumble, Mrs. Bloomer? Good, but you must not fail to inform Constable Potter if you suffer any after-effects. I am quite sure that Mrs. Potter will in any case independently describe to him what she has seen today. Where was I? Yes, well, I feel that we are all indebted to Miss Seeton for insuring that the meeting can now proceed without further interruptions. So without more ado, I call upon Miss Amelita Forby to speak to us."

Mel rose and grinned. "Madam Chairman, ladies. As you know, this talk was arranged at short notice, so I've only had time to throw together a few notes. And do you know what I planned as a working title? 'The Thrills and Spills of a Journalist's Life.' Well, I now realize that in comparison with you ladies, I have a very dull and uneventful time of it . . ."

chapter
~7~

“THAT’S ALL very fine and large, my dear chap,” Sir George Colveden argued, “but how can we keep the child from finding out what’s up if you fellers go trailing after her in your dirty great boots everywhere she goes?”

Chief Inspector Brinton looked miffed, for as a matter of fact he had surprisingly dainty feet for a man of his comfortable build. However, he held his tongue because the master of Rytham Hall was a golfing crony of his chief constable and therefore entitled to as many rhetorical questions as he liked.

“I mean, blue lights flashing, sirens, make way for the VIP type of thing, good Lord, she’s bound to twig. Not to mention the people in the streets. They don’t miss a trick, you know. Whereas if it’s just my son Nigel running her down in his MG to Eastbourne or Hastings or wherever it is she insists on going to practice, well, it’s just a young couple out for a spin, right? Mind you, I can’t for the life of me understand why her coach can’t come here. Our tennis court in the garden doesn’t get a lot of use and I seem to remember the net’s got a few holes in it, but—”

“No question of blue lights or anything like that, sir. I’m going along myself this first time. We’re in an unmarked car, in plain clothes. I'd be very surprised if your son notices us tucking in behind him. We'll keep our distance all right. Chief Constable's very insistent, sir, following a phone conversation with the commissioner at Scotland Yard."

Sir George was duly impressed. "Really? My word, top brass intervening personally, eh? Well, that's different, got to toe the line in that case, I s'pose. You'd better buzz off then, Brinton old boy, and lie in wait for the pair of 'em. I'm told young Patricia'll be down in a brace of shakes. I say, you should have seen the breakfast she tucked away. Fine healthy appetite, good breedin' stock by the look of those hips, if you want my opinion. That reminds me, goin' to the weddin', Brinton? Dr. Wright's girl and that young feller Ranger?"

"Hope to be at the church, General. Looking forward to it. By the way, Chief Superintendent Delphick's given Ranger a bit of extra leave beforehand to come down here and help his fiancée with the preparations. Be arriving later today, I understand . . ." Brinton paused, thinking that Sir George had something in his eye, but then realized that he was winking exaggeratedly.

"Nod's as good as a wink to a blind horse, Brinton. 'Nuff said. Extra pair of hands in case of need, what? Quite agree, can't be too careful. All the same, we're all well and truly on the *qui vive* here, you know. Had to let my wife and Nigel in on the secret just before Patricia got here, naturally, but they've promised to keep mum. Anybody trying any hanky-panky while young Thumper's girl's under my roof'll regret it, take my word for it."

"Do stop waffling, Nigel, there's a dear. I'm trying to concentrate."

Nigel Colveden flushed with pleasure and gulped. He was inured to being accused of waffling, and almost always shut up obediently when told to. Mind you, a person had good reason to waffle a bit when experiencing the high privilege and awesome responsibility of driving Trish Thumper to Hastings, there to deliver her into the custody of her coach. Especially in view of what Dad had told him and Ma the previous day, before that frightful old father of hers had driven her down to Rytham Hall and, thank goodness, beetled off again after being closeted for half an hour with Dad in the library.

But for her to say "there's a dear" to him! To N. P. R. Colveden in person! While sitting in all her bounteous glory an inch or two away, smelling most deliciously of soap. Gosh, you can keep your Chanel Number Five. My Fabulous Pink Camay Girl, he thought to himself rapturously, fumbling the change down into third gear but slowing down to a crawl beside the church in good time to allow the driver of the brewery lorry outside the George and Dragon to pull away. Good to know the suppliers of Watney's Fine Ales were on the job, and that, come opening time, thirsty patrons wouldn't be disappointed.

"Well, well, well," Norman observed to Harvey, who had just emerged from the church and joined him in the porch. "That, 'Arve, is what I call a turn-up for the book. See what I see?"

Harvey glanced in the direction indicated, and then hurriedly drew back into the shadows. "Horrors! Do me a favor, Norman, I've got a weak heart."

"Got it in one, my son, dunno abaht yer ticker but glad yer eyesight's all right. Three members of the Old Bill in an unmarked car, or I'm the Queen of Sheba, no offense intended, 'Arvey. Funny how you can always tell, innit? Honest, they might just as well stick a neon sign on top. Three big geezers like that . . ."

"It's dreadful to behold. What the heck are they doing in a dreary little place like this?"

"Ah, you may well ask. But don't get all of a doodah, me lad, I don't think it's 'cos they've rumbled us. It's more intrestin' than that. What I saw an' you didn't was the little red MG what went by just previous. Bet you a quid them fuzz is doin' an escort job, 'Arvey, an' you'll never guess 'oo they're mindin'." Norman grinned at his companion, who winced and averted his eyes from the display of discolored teeth. "That bird."

"Really, Norman, you can be absolutely maddening sometimes, you know. What bird?"

"Ol' Thumper's kid. The tennis player. I seen 'er play the other day, thought I reckernized 'er. Seein' the Old Bill trailin' along be'ind makes it a cert."

"Really, such imagination! Out of the question. I've heard of her, but she's not all that famous, not enough to rate a police escort."

Norman winked conspiratorially. "Oh, I dunno. Bet you somethin', my gloomy ol' pal Bill Parsons'll crack a smile when I tell 'im."

"Never. He's incapable of such a thing. Why should he, anyway?"

"Never you mind. You finished in there?"

"Yes. It'll be a doddle. The lock on the silver cupboard in the vestry's a joke, ditto the one on the side door. I tell you, if we had a couple of suitcases and some old newspapers handy, I'd be tempted to do the job here and now."

"More 'aste less speed, 'Arvey. Never know 'oo might be in an' out this time o' day. Nah, ternight's the night, when ev'rybody's 'ome watchin' the telly or in the pub an' we can button up all three jobs nice an' tidy. Bill's comin' on parade at 'arf past eight."

• • •

Miss Seeton was ever so slightly tipsy, and pottering about in her little kitchen in the twilight, clearing up after her visitors. How good it had been of Anne and Mr. Ranger to drop in to see her, and how very fortunate that she had a nearly half-full bottle of sherry in the house and could drink their health with them. They'd gone slightly soft and limp, the cream crackers, that is, but they were more suitable to accompany sherry than the Bath Olivers in the biscuit barrel would have been. Who had Oliver been, one wondered, and what had been his connection with Bath? Not Cromwell, surely, he had scarcely been the sort of man one would presume to name a biscuit after.

Whereas Sally Lunn, though perhaps a little immodest in doing so, had been perfectly entitled to apply her own name to her recipe. Like seedsmen who produce new hybrid roses, or clematis, or . . . oh, all sorts of things. Perhaps Sally Lunn had invented Bath buns, too. But presumably not Bath chairs, or those funny little ham things. Bath chaps.

Interesting that men were often referred to as chaps, too. Mr. Ranger—Bob, one really must try to get used to calling him that, now that he was about to become dear Anne's husband—had used the expression on looking at the sketches she had made after watching the tennis at the Hurlingham Club. Peculiar looking chaps, he had said about her cartoons of Sir Wilfred Thumper and the St. John's Ambulance man. Then, how typically of dear Bob, explained that he hadn't meant to be impolite about her drawings, which he thought were jolly good, of course.

Miss Seeton looked at the sherry bottle, in which less than half an inch remained. She was almost sure she had taken only the one small glass herself, though in the excitement of talking about the wedding next week it might possibly have been two. Anyway, it seemed rather silly to keep such a small amount. With careful deliberation she poured it into her glass and to her own surprise disposed of half of it in a single gulp. Then the phone rang in the living room, and she made her way a little unsteadily toward it, sinking gratefully into an easy chair and blinking at the receiver which was making little squawking noises.

"Wrong number," she said to it eventually. It seemed the simplest thing to do in the circumstances.

"Miss Seeton? That is you, surely? This is Molly Treeves. At the vicarage."

Miss Seeton was not so far gone as to be beyond recall, and Miss Treeves's crisply authoritative tones acted upon her like a cold damp towel. She continued to have a little trouble with her tongue, but otherwise pulled herself together very creditably.

"Oh dear. Do apologize, Mystery. I mean Miss Treev*zer*."

"You are quite well, are you? I haven't interrupted your yoga practice?"

"No, no, no," Miss Seeton assured her, and then, to make herself absolutely clear, added a few more nos.

"It's about the church flowers this week, you see," Miss Treeves went on, somewhat hesitantly for her. "It's your turn, as I'm sure you know."

"Flowers? My turn? If you say so, must be so." In spite of becoming dimly aware that a headache was flexing its muscles somewhere not far away and getting ready to pounce, Miss Seeton still felt euphoric enough to tackle this unexpected hurdle.

"Splendid. It's just that Arthur was hoping you might be good enough to get them done fairly early tomorrow. By about ten, perhaps? The Archdeacon's due to arrive to carry out his visitation at eleven, so naturally Arthur wants the place to look its best."

"Quite understand. Quite. Quite. Wouldn't dream of letting vicar down. Got to marry Anne and Bob next week, after all."

By the time she finally put the phone down, Miss Seeton had sobered up almost completely, it having dawned on her that she had planned to catch the early bus to Brettenden the next morning, in order to buy a couple of sketching pads and some more charcoal at the little shop where they sold basic artist's materials as well as simple sheet music, cheap plastic recorders, and "kits for creative craftspersons."

Never mind. One would simply have to get up an hour earlier than usual, that's all. And though one could hardly gather from the garden and arrange the necessary flowers and greenery in the dark, there was no reason why one shouldn't do a little planning in advance, by just popping along to the church with a flashlight and reminding oneself of the size, number, and location of the vases to be filled. Never put off till tomorrow what you can do today, had been one of the admirable Victorian precepts drummed into her in childhood, and Emily D. Seeton decided that she was perfectly capable of doing that much before bedtime.

chapter

–8–

"THERE'S ICE cream," the lone waitress announced, inopportunely appearing at their table just as Mel thought she had detected an encouragingly fond, even speculative look in Thrudd Banner's eye. Since the failure of Mr. Pontefract's quick-snack bar, an ill-conceived enterprise save for its catchy name *Bits 'n' Pizzas*, the George and Dragon's own dining room was Plummergen's sole restaurant. It was hardly a mecca for gastronomes, but Mel was enjoying herself all the same.

Thrudd had turned up around six as promised, and joined her in the bar for a couple of drinks after checking in and taking a shower: an experience he described most amusingly. Speculation as to why British showerheads never seemed to produce more than a dismal trickle in comparison with the Niagaralike torrents of the American version carried them through the first drink, by which time the alcohol had loosened Mel's tongue sufficiently for her to embark on a spirited account of the afternoon's eventful Women's Institute meeting that lasted through the second.

Chatting about Thrudd's visit to Bonn had helped to soften the impact of the George and Dragon's prawn cocktail followed by overdone beef and soggy vegetables, but the bottle of eminently drinkable claret Thrudd ordered had done much more toward generating their present expansive mood.

"What kind?" Thrudd inquired of the waitress, genially enough. The girl, whose name was Maureen and who was anxious to get rid of them, clear up, and join her boyfriend Wayne who had a Kawasaki motorbike, gazed at him in bafflement.

"Beg pardon?"

"I mean, what flavors do you have?"

Maureen shrugged. "Just ice cream. Ordinary ice cream. You know, no flavor."

"Ah." Thrudd nodded sagely. "No flavor. Sounds delicious. Could be vanilla, Mel. Want some?"

Mel shook her head with a grin. "Better not. Two scoops of vanilla ice and I'm anybody's. Just coffee."

"Okay. No ice cream, thanks. Just two coffees. Bring them to us in the saloon bar, would you?"

Judging by the expression on Maureen's face, she regarded such an unconventional request as being positively Babylonian in its outrageousness, and with tightly compressed lips she disappeared through the service door. Soon Thrudd and Mel were ensconced once more in the bar, each with a double cognac, and not really interested in the coffee Thrudd had ordered. This was as well, because after thinking about it Maureen had decided that life was quite complicated enough as it was, and had gone off duty.

"So. Apart from Miss S.'s heroic achievement in revealing Erica Nuttel's scanties to the world, what else is new in swinging Plummergen?"

Mel pondered briefly before replying. "Hard to know where to start, really. Anne Wright and Bob Ranger are getting married here next week, and that's the main topic of interest in the village." Her eyes glistened reminiscently. "Or was, at least, until the row this afternoon. Oddly enough the word about Trish Thumper staying with the Colvedens doesn't seem to have got round yet. Even though young Nigel's floating around grinning like an idiot at everybody he meets. He looks like that character in *Mad* magazine. Alfred E. Neumann, isn't it?''

''Nigel always looks like Alfred E. Neumann when he's in love,'' Thrudd pointed out, ''which is most of the time. As for Trish, not everybody reads the sports pages, you know, and she isn't exactly in the Margaret Court or Billie Jean King league. The important thing is, have you dug up anything else on these allegations about her old man?''

''Not so far,'' Mel admitted. ''Miss S. more or less repeated them cheerfully enough when I went to see her, but you know how she keeps going off on a tangent. I hardly like to waylay the vicar and ask him. I mean, for heaven's sake, Thrudd, he might be involved himself. Unmarried middle-aged clergymen are forever getting into the Sunday papers.''

''Yes, but choirboys are their downfall as a rule,'' Thrudd said with a great air of well-informed authority. ''Can't see the vicar of Plummergen snuggling up to Mr. Justice Thumper, somehow.'' He looked at his watch. ''Look, it's hardly nine-fifteen. What say we take a little stroll as far as the vicarage, see if he's home? If he is, chat about this and that in a casual sort of way, and see what comes of it?''

All the talk about snuggling up had pointed Mel's thoughts in quite a different direction, like upstairs, but she remembered that Molly Treeves had, in thanking her privately after the end of the meeting, cordially invited her to drop in at the vicarage at any time. It might well be diverting to follow up Thrudd's idea. She swallowed the last of her brandy too quickly, spluttered, and dabbed at her watering eyes. Then she got up and stood looking down at him. Tonight, she suddenly decided, was going to be the night.

If T. Banner didn't make a move, she would. But there'd be no harm in strolling along to the vicarage first.

"Okay, you dynamic newshound, we'll go dig up some dirt. On your feet!"

The evening air was balmy and fragrant, and Miss Seeton breathed deeply of it as she strolled toward the church, her long, heavy flashlight in her hand but switched off. It was almost dark, but one could still make out the shapes of the buildings in The Street, of a car parked a little beyond the churchyard lych-gate, and the illuminated sign outside the George and Dragon. The incipient headache was still there in the background, but it no longer seemed inevitable that it would prevail, and Miss Seeton began to sing to herself. She had a good memory for tunes and rhythms, but a poor one for words, and rarely managed a complete line.

Thus it was that, having denuded the vestry cupboard of the silver it contained and while Harvey was relocking it, he and Norman were startled to hear the heavy latch on the west door rattle, the door itself squeak open, and a small but jaunty voice singing "A *wand*'ring minstrel I, a thing of *tum*ty tumty . . ." And then desist, as though it had suddenly occurred to its owner that though the psalmist had stressed that it was perfectly in order to sing unto God with the voice of melody, that probably wasn't the sort of melody he'd had in mind.

"Cripes," Norman whispered. "Oo the 'ell's that?" One must be charitable and give him the benefit of the doubt at this point. In the course of numerous appearances before magistrates over the years, it had been pointed out more than once to Norman that his chosen career involved a deplorably slack attitude toward the eighth commandment. It may however be questioned whether he realized that his words on this occasion put him in breach of the third, too. On a technicality.

Harvey hastily doused the tiny pocket torch he had been using, while Norman peeped round the half-open vestry door just as Miss Seeton switched on her flashlight and its powerful beam stabbed through the darkness of the nave. Never having had occasion previously to note the location of the electric light switches in the church, Miss Seeton directed the beam here and there more or less at random, until it picked out the cross on the altar in such a splendidly theatrical way that she held it in that position for a time while she admired the effect.

It was, she decided, a bit like the climax of a production of *Aida* she had seen at the Sadler's Wells Theatre in north London one evening at the end of the Second World War, when the fog outside was so dense that it pervaded the auditorium and lent an unearthly radiance to the spotlights on . . . who had it been? Victoria Sladen? A very *large* diva, anyway.

But come, this would never do. Miss Seeton abandoned the idea of trying to find the light switches, and proceeded up the central aisle, trying to recall the last occasion when she had been responsible for the flowers, and where she had put them. There were the two big vases, one on either side just inside the communion rail. Some of the day lilies from her garden would do very well for those, but the big shallow bowl on the shelf just below the ledge of the pulpit was going to be more of a problem . . .

Her musings were disturbed by a muffled clanking noise coming from the direction of the vestry, and for the first time since setting out from Sweetbriars Miss Seeton experienced a flicker of unease. She pointed her torch toward the vestry, the door of which she then saw was ajar.

"Vicar? Er, is that you, Mr. Treeves? Mr. Treeooblh—"

Having left the church door open, she had not heard William Parsons enter behind her. Parsons himself was in a state of indecision. He had been given specific instructions to remain at the wheel of the getaway car outside the church, but none about what he should do if, while his colleagues in crime were about their business, he glanced at the rear-view mirror and saw a slightly built, elderly lady approach, go in through the lych-gate, and make for the church door. Something had to be done, though, so he had quietly followed her, watched her movements and then temporarily lost his head and pounced when she called out. With his hand now clamped firmly over her mouth, he could keep the old girl reasonably quiet, but that left only one of his arms free to try to control her furious and surprisingly agile struggles, and for crying out loud, watch out for that damn flashlight . . .

It was too late. The impact of the heavy torch on the side of his head just above his right ear was not only violent enough to jar the bulb and extinguish the light, it also stunned William Parsons, who sank to his knees as Miss Seeton wriggled free, only to be grabbed again by Norman, who dragged her unbuttoned cardigan off her shoulders and used it to tie her wrists together behind her before she realized what was happening. Then he pushed her face down to the cold stone slabs of the floor of the nave and unceremoniously sat on her behind. And just when one had been on the point of apologizing for hitting the other person with the torch! It had been the man's own fault, of course, and he and his friends were clearly up to no good, but one did so hate violence. There seemed to be little point in reasoning with them, so one might as well just wait and see . . .

"Switch that bloody thing off!" Norman hissed to Harvey, whose little pocket flashlight had briefly illuminated the scene. "An' keep your gobs zipped up, both of yer.

Wake up, dumbbell, you're not 'urt, move it . . . give us your tie. Necktie.'' Deeply embarrassed by the results of his intervention and still woozy from the effects of the blow to his head, Parsons clumsily pulled off his tie and held it out in the direction of Norman's voice. A few seconds later, Miss Seeton's ankles had been tied together, but her captor remained where he was for the time being.

''Right, scarper! Out front an' get that stuff stowed away. I'll be right wivyer!''

Only after she had heard the other two men leave the church was the crushing weight on her removed, and Miss Seeton heard herself being addressed directly for the first time.

''Right, listen to me, lady. Dunno 'oo you are or what the 'ell you're up to, but you're dead lucky, you are. An' if you wanter stay lucky, you jus' lie there nice an' quiet an' count up to a thousand 'fore you even think about yellin', or tryin' to get yourself undone. You let me down we shall know it, sure as a gun, an' one o' the boys'll be back one fine day to sort yer out.''

''Somebody's in a hurry,'' Thrudd Banner remarked, grabbing Mel by the upper arm and pulling her back from the curb as a car hurtled down The Street from the direction of the church and disappeared round the corner at the end. ''Damn fool roadhogs, only their sidelights on, too.'' He released her arm, and Mel promptly slipped it back through his as they crossed the now deserted road and turned right.

''You sure it isn't too late to bother the Treeveses? Doubt if Plummergen folk are nightbirds, somehow.'' Mel gave Thrudd's arm a hopeful little squeeze. And wasn't that a little return pressure? ''It's a nice evening. Why don't we just wander about for a while and then call it a day ourselves?''

"Okay by me. Unless the vicarage is a blaze of light when we get there, and Molly Treeves is out on the doorstep looking out for another couple to make up a four for bridge."

They ambled along in companionable silence for a while before Thrudd spoke again. "Fascinating when you come to think of it."

"What is?"

"The way the upper classes stick together. I mean, if old Wilfred Thumper really is that way inclined, you'd have thought there'd have been rumors over the years. Specially about a guy with a public reputation like his. Thing is, what are you proposing to do about it if it turns out to be true?"

"Search me. An item like that'd be bound to come in handy sooner or later, though. Waste not, want not, that's my motto." She stopped abruptly. "Ssh, listen. Can you hear somebody calling out?"

"Where?"

"Sort of high-pitched. Seems to be coming from the church."

"Probably a cat. Forget it."

"Don't think so. We're going that way anyway. Even if it is only a cat, we ought to let the poor thing out."

By the time Mel and Thrudd neared the lych-gate, the sound was clearly audible, and could not possibly have been made by a cat. In fact they soon identified it, and rushed to the west door, which was partly open. They expected to find Miss Seeton inside, but not in a contorted heap on the floor attempting with wrists tied behind her to reach her similarly bound ankles.

chapter 9

"SHE REALLY is a remarkably resilient person for her age," Dr. Wright said when he came downstairs, followed by his daughter, and the others looked up at him expectantly. "Or, to put it another way, she's as tough as an old boot. I tried several times to persuade her to spend the night at the nursing home just to be on the safe side, but she wouldn't hear of it. Anne will bear me out."

"Quite right," Anne confirmed, gazing fondly at Bob Ranger, who was overfilling an easy chair while Mel Forby and Thrudd Banner occupied the sofa in the living room at Sweetbriars. "She'd got the idea into her head that we're much too busy with the arrangements for the wedding to want her underfoot, as she put it."

"But she really is okay, is she, Doctor?"

"A number of bruises and contusions from dragging herself over the stone floor to the church door, but nothing serious, no. And fortunately she'd worked herself up into such a high old state of indignation over the way the men behaved that she quite forgot to go into shock. The sedative I put in her cocoa will give her a good night's sleep, and apart from a few aches and pains, she should be as right as rain in the morning." He switched his medical bag from one hand to the other and looked round the room benignly. "Well, I'll be off, then, it's past my bedtime. Leave you young people to it. You'll look in on Miss Seeton first thing in the morning then, Anne. Look her over, help her dress and so forth, right? Fine. 'Night, all."

"I'm wondering if I ought to kip down on the sofa for the night," Bob said thoughtfully after his prospective father-in-law had left. "PC Potter's reported the incident to Ashford, and they'll be sending a CID man over to talk to Miss S. in the morning . . ."

Thrudd grinned. "So naturally you want a piece of the action, right?"

"I should jolly well think he does," Anne said stoutly. "Miss Seeton's a consultant to Scotland Yard, and don't you forget it."

Thrudd threw up his hands in mock defensiveness. "I surrender, don't hit me again, lady. Might be a good idea at that, though I can't really see these desperadoes coming back to have another go at her, can you?"

"What beats me is how she managed to get herself to the door tied up like that in the dark *and* wriggle herself up against it backwards to lift that heavy latch," Mel said, and Anne nodded in agreement.

"Thank goodness she did, though, or she might have been lying there all night. Nobody could possibly have heard her calling out if the door had stayed closed."

"I'm telling you, even at that it was darn close to a miracle that Thrudd and I were near enough to the church to hear her. And we still haven't figured out what in the world she was doing there in the first place. You know how it is with Miss S., she was gassing away nineteen to the dozen while we were untying her, but she hasn't got the knack of finishing one sentence before she gets involved in explaining something else entirely. What was all that about *Aida* and doing the flowers, Thrudd?"

"Ask me another." He yawned mightily. "The poor old girl'd been through a pretty rough half hour, after all. She'll probably make better sense in the morning. You going to stay here or not, Bob? If you are, we'll walk Anne home and then head for the pub."

"But what on earth am I to say to the Archdeacon?" the Reverend Arthur Treeves moaned for the third time since PC Potter had taken his leave and promised to return in the morning with a colleague from Ashford to take down the details of the stolen silver.

His sister snorted. Characters in books are often described as snorting when in fact the sound envisaged is probably more like an explosive, contemptuous, or mirthless laugh, which would come out as "Hah!" in direct speech. Still flushed with her triumph over Erica Nuttel at the Women's Institute meeting earlier that day, Molly Treeves really snorted; to such effect that she hastily had recourse to the box of Kleenex conveniently at hand.

"Well, for goodness sake, don't apologize to him, whatever you do. Blame the churchwardens," she then advised. "It's all their fault anyway, I expect, and there's nothing the Archdeacon can do to them. Pull yourself together, do. It isn't as if you took the blessed silver and tied Miss Seeton up. The Nuts are much more likely suspects, in view of the fact that Miss Seeton pulled Erica Nuttel's trousers down this afternoon."

This was the first the vicar had heard of the imbroglio, and he goggled in amazement. "My dear Molly, you can't mean, that is you aren't seriously suggesting . . ."

"Oh, go to bed, Arthur. I'll talk to your precious Archdeacon for you if you're too feeble."

• • •

"Gawd, I don't never want no more excitement like that," Norman announced, and then added a couple more negatives to ram his point home. "Not never."

Harvey said nothing, but shuddered delicately and raised his glass of pink gin in mute agreement before drinking deeply. William Parsons remained slumped in his chair, a very picture of despair. It was just after one-thirty in the morning, and the three men were in the living room of Norm's unexpectedly snug flat above the Jade Garden, a Chinese take-away restaurant in South London's Lewisham High Street, a safe hour-and-a-half's drive from the scenes of their recent exploits.

"Still, there in't no need to sit there lookin' like a pregnant duck, even if you did upset the apple cart an' get a wallop on your bonce for interferin', Bill. Give us a tune on that ol' fiddle-face, blimey, we done all three jobs as per accordin' to plan in the end, din't we?"

"I think you were out of your tiny mind to insist on going ahead with the other two after that ghastly business in Plummergen, if you want my opinion. My nerves were in *shreds*."

"You're up the pole, 'Arve. Why, even if that ol' bird 'ad managed to get out o' there an' kick up a rumpus in less than an hour, you're not tellin' me the Old Bill would go tearin' round the neighbor'ood lookin' for us in other *churches*, are yer? Nah, we was as safe as 'ouses on them other jobs."

Parsons was not so easily to be cheered. "I feel terrible. That old woman could easily have had a heart attack, thanks to me. Don't you realize she might be dead, with the police setting up a murder hunt for us at this very moment? And even if she is all right, she's a *witness*, Norm. My God,

I'd never have got into this if I'd imagined for a moment that . . ."

"Blimey, 'ark 'oo's talkin'! Don't you come the old acid with me, Bill. What you got in mind on yer own account in't no Sunday school outin'. Far as tonight went, first place, that ol' biddy weren't no shrinkin' violet. She as near as dammit 'ad you out for the count there. An' I felt the muscles on 'er when I was fixin' 'er up. I'll give you two 'undred to one she's back 'ome sinkin a glass or two to settle 'er tum, just like us. Second place, there in't no way she could've got a make on us." He chuckled. "Unless o' course you 'ad your name an' address embroidered on that tie o' yours."

"No. It was a birthday present, years ago," Parsons admitted, and unexpectedly brushed a tear from the corner of his eye. "It probably came from Woolworths."

"Well, then, there you are. You listen to me, mate, the on'y one of us what 'as anythin' to worry about's me, 'cause I'm the on'y one she 'eard say anythin', an' I never used no names. So if I'm sayin' we done all right tonight, we done all right. Get it?" He pointed at the collection of silver candlesticks, chalices, collection plates, and other items ranged on the table. "All we want now is for 'Arvey to wangle us the right price for this little lot—an' 'e chose 'em so 'e knows where ter place 'em—an' we'll all be laughin'. Specially you, Bill Parsons."

"Why me?"

"Why you? I'll tell you why. We got a bit o' good news for you, me ol' mate. Bin savin' it up for the occasion. Abaht that certain person you're interested in, namin' no names, know what I mean?" Norman winked prodigiously. "Well, guess 'oo spotted 'is daughter the tennis whizz this mornin'—" he glanced at the clock on the mantelpiece and corrected himself, "I mean yes'dy mornin'. In a little MG bein' driven by a young feller, an' trailed by a carload o' fuzz?'' Norman blew on his fingernails and polished them ostentatiously on his lapel. ''Yours truly is 'oo. Minders, them rozzers in the car be'ind was. So later on we nosed round a bit, 'Arve an' me. Turns out the car belongs to a Nigel Colveden, son an' heir of Sir George Colveden of Rytham 'All, just outside Plummergen. An' that's where your ol' sparrin' partner's kid's bin stashed away for safe keepin'. Oho! Penny beginnin' to drop, is it? Cheerin' up a bit, are we, then? Thought that might put the roses back in them pale chops o' yours . . . ''

A little later, Bob Ranger shifted uneasily on Miss Seeton's sofa. It was much too short for him to stretch out on it, but by pulling one of the easy chairs alongside to accommodate the lower part of his legs when bent at the knees, he had contrived to start off reasonably comfortably. The problem was that whenever he wanted to turn over—and in defiance of common sense he kept doing so in the hope of achieving a better fit—he had to move the easy chair along to the other end. At some stage it had occurred to him to bring up the second chair, but the acrobatics subsequently involved in reversing his position woke him up so thoroughly that he decided with a sigh to give up the struggle and do a bit of thinking.

He devoted some time to wistful daydreaming about the new king-sized bed he expected to be sharing with Anne after they returned from their honeymoon and took up residence in the house they were buying with the aid of a ten-thousand-pound building society loan in Bromley, within easy commuting distance of London, and not all that far from Plummergen by car. Too far for Anne to be able to go on working for her father as nurse/receptionist, unfortunately; but she already had a job lined up in Bromley as secretary to a group medical practice, and Dr. Wright had found a redoubtable lady, a recently retired Army nursing officer who liked to be addressed as Major Howett and seemed certain to become known as The Howitzer, to run his private nursing home for him.

What with Anne's salary and his metropolitan police sergeant's pay and allowances, they ought to be able to manage pretty well, at least until . . . well, they'd have to cross that bridge when they came to it, wouldn't they? The main thing was to get this blessed wedding over with and push off on aforesaid honeymoon before the Oracle had a chance to get it into his noddle that the Thumper blackmailing affair and Miss Seeton's latest adventure required his continuing presence in Plummergen.

Not, of course, that the two cases were in any way related. It was just that if there was trouble around, Miss S. headed straight for it like a blooming homing pigeon. She really did get up to some barmy tricks, like deciding to go pottering about the church in the dark just when a bunch of villains were helping themselves to the communion plate. Pity she hadn't got there soon enough to scare them off, then the police needn't have been involved at all. As it was, old Potter had had the time of his life, bothering the vicar, then on the phone to his divisional HQ reporting the burglary and the assault on Miss S. The moment Chief Inspector Brinton heard about it, he'd be bound to descend on Plummergen to take personal charge, *and* be on the blower toot sweet to the Oracle, and . . .

Filled with forboding and convinced that he was in for a wakeful, depressing night, Detective Sergeant Bob Ranger drifted into a deep, dreamless sleep.

Upstairs in her own bed, Miss Seeton was also asleep, but unlike her protector below was dreaming energetically.

Of a spotlit Aida center stage and visibly growing larger, waving her arms about and brandishing a tennis racket, with Bellini's doge looking sorrowfully on, and . . . someone else in shadow, but the shadow turned to blackness and there was pressure, pressure, but then it was gone again and, absurdly, Nigel was proffering a bouquet of day lilies not to Aida but to the doge . . . and yes, of course!

Miss Seeton's eyes snapped open for a few seconds. Of course, *that* was who it was!

Then she went back to sleep.

Upstairs in the George and Dragon, Thrudd Banner was nearly asleep, again, but Mel Forby had managed to revive him twice already with a certain amount of imagination and ingenuity, and had no intention of desisting for quite some time. The past couple of hours had been altogether too delicious. Starting with the nightcap in his room, from his bottle of duty-free Dimple Haig with water from the tap, in tooth-glasses. Followed by a speculative look from him, a teasing insult and a slap on the wrist from her, warm, strong hands seizing both of hers, a playful bout of wrestling that fooled neither of them, and then the first fierce, aggressive kiss, the breaking away, the wide-eyed, wondering gaze of mutual realization turning to one of open desire . . . and then at last the heart-thudding joy of that long-awaited naked embrace, the impossibility of ever getting enough of each other!

At least, that was the way she, Amelita Forby, saw the situation, and without more ado she set to work to persuade Thrudd that, in bed at least, it is equally blessed both to give and to receive.

chapter

–10–

CHIEF INSPECTOR Chris Brinton looked at the cupboard in the vestry in disgust and disbelief, sniffed, and turned to Detective Constable Foxon. "Dunno why they didn't just keep the stuff in a wet paper bag. Even you could've sprung that lock. With one of your hair-curlers." Foxon scowled defensively.

"Leave it off, Guv. So what if it is a bit long? Matter of fact, I had an appointment at Charlene's Unisex Snip 'n' Blow this morning, and whose fault is it I couldn't keep it, Sir?" It being Saturday, Brinton decided that a degree of mutinous behavior was allowable, and let the impertinence pass.

"All right, all right, let's get on. It looks like turning into a right sort of shambles today anyway, without you and me giving each other any aggro."

There were standing orders at Ashford divisional police headquarters that Brinton was to be informed, if necessary by telephone at home, of any incident in Plummergen or involving Miss Seeton. Mercifully on this occasion the news had reached him after rather than during a tender half-hour with Mrs. Brinton, and he had taken a certain satisfaction in ringing up the Oracle at home just before midnight to put him in the picture.

At that stage the burglaries at two other churches within ten miles of Plummergen had not yet been reported. News of one had come in by the time Brinton and Foxon left Ashford, and they learned of the other over the car radio on the way.

"What time's Mr. Delphick s'posed to get here?"

"Eleven or so, he said. He'll pick up Ranger from the doctor's place and find us. Then we'll all have a word with Miss S., bite to eat at the pub after, and then you'd better get your backside over to the other two villages, unless we get word of more of the same, in which case we'll very likely need to call in the US Cavalry."

Brinton gazed gloomily round the vestry, plucked a surplice off a hook behind the door, and held it up against himself. "Not sure I fancy going to heaven if regulation dress is anything like this." He put it back. "There's a dabs team doing the rounds, fat chance they've got. I ask you, three, count them, at least three jobs during the same night in the same area. Has to be the same villain behind them, right, Foxon?"

"Offering me a bet, sir? I'd chance a couple of quid on it."

"Big of you. So would everybody else. You'd think something like that'd be a dabs man's delight. Find just one print common to all three places and there you go. Pull off a series of jobs like that, cheeky sods are bound to be pros, very likely got some form, bingo. No trouble finding the right collars to feel. But whoever tried isolating a fingerprint in a *church*, for crying out loud? Might just as well run your dusting brush over Waterloo Station."

"Right. And if they did get lucky and come up with a common print, it'd very likely turn out to be the bishop's."

"Talking of bishops, who's the bigwig the vicar said he had to rush back to his house to meet?"

"Archdeacon. Not sure exactly where he fits in, sir. Got a vague idea he's some sort of bishop's adjutant or admin officer. They're the blokes who get clobbered by the opposition whenever they sell off some rundown old church to be turned into a Macdonalds hamburger bar, anyway."

"Ah. You know, you sometimes surprise me with your erudition, Foxon. Well, if he's in for a bollocking, no wonder old Treeves was looking like a dying duck in a thunderstorm. On the other hand, from what you say, this archdeacon chap might prefer the insurance money to the silver whatnots . . . my word, it'll be a turnup for the book if we uncover a ring of bent clergymen nicking their own stuff, wouldn't it?"

". . . so I thought I'd just look in and ask you how things seem to be going, sir."

"And jolly nice it is to see you, Delphick old boy. Everything shipshape and Bristol fashion so far, I'm glad to say. Nigel's in his seventh heaven chauffeuring the girl back and forth to wherever it is she insists on going, and she seems happy enough. Not a lot to say for herself, mind you, but judging by the amount she puts away at mealtimes, she's not pining away." Sir George Colveden fondled his moustache for a moment, his expression darkening. "Bad business about Miss Seeton, though, what? Things have come to a shockin' pass when a lady can't even drop into her parish church with a handful of flowers without a bunch of ruffians assaulting her."

"I haven't spoken to her myself yet, but Sergeant Ranger rang me before I left home this morning and I gathered from him that she seems to have given a pretty good account of herself. And that she seems to be quite chirpy today after a good night's sleep."

"As one would expect, my dear chap, just as one would expect of her. Miss Seeton is one of the old school, you see." Sir George nodded complacently, not unaware that any fair-minded person of his acquaintance would say the same thing about him. "My wife said she'll pop in and see her later today. Take her a pot of jam or something, though what a person recovering after a nasty experience needs with jam I fail to grasp. Anyway, we were talking about young Thumper's daughter. Getting anywhere, are you? Tracking down the bounder behind those disgraceful letters, I mean."

Delphick pursed his lips and breathed out through his nose. "Depends how you look at it. For want of any positive leads, we've had to proceed on what seems to be the only commonsense theory, that the letters were sent by an ex-convict with a grudge against Sir Wilfred. Somebody released at about the time the letters began to arrive. Now as a magistrate, you're aware that the Home Office is awash with statistics about all manner of unlikely things—"

"Proportion of left-handed forgers with red hair in the criminal population, that sort of nonsense? Quite. But you're going to tell me that when you asked for a simple little thing like a list of chaps sent down by Wilfred Thumper . . ."

"Precisely, sir." Not for the first time it occurred to Delphick that Sir George wasn't as daft as he often sounded. "They were, to put it tactfully, less than helpful."

"Civil servants? Jumped up, blitherin' idiots for the most part. Know what I do when I have to write to one, Delphick? At the bottom I put 'You are, Sir, My obedient servant, G. Colveden.' Doesn't do a bit of good mind you, but I like to make the point. So you had to send chaps beetling round all Her Majesty's prisons, did you? Have a look at their discharge logs?''

''Bang on again, General. I can see I ought to have consulted you from the first. And there's been a lot of delving in the records of the Royal Courts of Justice. Anyway, to cut a long and tedious story short, we did manage to draw up a list. And we've been able to eliminate a good many of the names with reasonable confidence. On the other hand, we're a long way from having a particular suspect in our sights, and of course we might very well be on the wrong track altogether.''

''Every confidence in you, me dear fellow. And Brinton, of course,'' Sir George added charitably after a perceptible pause, ''who is presumably after these blighters who mistreated Miss Seeton. Brinton's inclined to be a bit of a bull in a china shop in my experience, but then there's no need for overmuch subtlety in handling gentry like these, I s'pose. As I shall make crystal clear to them if they come up before me in due course, I can assure you. Now where was I? Ah, yes, Brinton. Can't say I'm sorry if he's otherwise engaged at present, between you and me and the gatepost he's been rather overdoin' the bodyguard act on Patricia. Carloads of flatfoots pursuin' her and Nigel every time they go out of the gate. I say, I've just remembered, we're all supposed to go over to this fancy opera place next Tuesday, Glyndebourne is it? Thumper's treat, perfectly frightful prospect. Well, I'm not having Brinton's merry men on parade that evening, I can tell you . . .''

''Oh dear, Mr. Delphick, I do feel so very embarrassed over the trouble I've caused everybody, especially poor Mr. Ranger, that is, Bob, as I am trying to remember to call him.''

Seeing one of his superior's eyebrows rise, Ranger

cleared his throat noisily. "It's nothing, sir. Just a bit of a crick in the neck from sleeping on Miss Seeton's sofa—"

"So very generous and thoughtful, though I'm sure I wasn't really in need of protection, because the gentleman—why I refer to him in that way I really can't imagine—the *person* who spoke to me did explain that he and his friends would come back to, er, complain only if I called out before counting to a thousand, and it took me much longer than that. Because of breaking my torch when I hit the other man, you see. To find my way to the door, that is, and unlatch it."

"You're sure there were three men altogether, Miss Seeton?"

"Quite sure, Mr. Brinton. The one who came up behind me when I called out to the vicar, only it wasn't the vicar, of course, and now that I think about it I realize that Mr. Treeves would be most unlikely to drop things in the dark in the vestry instead of putting the light on. As indeed I should have done myself had I known where the switches were. But then I would have missed the striking effect of the crucifix illuminated in the beam of my torch, wouldn't I? And the two who came out to help him after I hit him—" Miss Seeton paused in apparent embarrassment and briefly wrung her hands. "You know, I should so much like to be able to say that the blow was unintentional, but I fear—"

"Good gracious, you're surely not wasting sympathy on a man who assaulted you, are you?"

"Well, no, his behavior was certainly deplorable, and at the time of course I had no way of knowing that I'd seen him before—"

"You *what*? Sorry, I didn't mean to shout at you."

"That's perfectly all right, Mr. Brinton," she said primly, making Brinton feel thoroughly ashamed of himself and rephrase his question in a hushed, almost reverent voice. "May I just confirm this? Did I understand you to say that you can identify at least one of the men who were in the church last night?"

"Well, I don't know who he is, but I saw him at the tennis match."

Delphick intervened. "Would that be the tennis match you went to in London, Miss Seeton?"

"With the Treeveses and Nigel, yes. Sir Wilfred and Lady Thumper were there, too, I saw him as Bellini's doge, strong-willed but at the same time curiously wistful, you know. Whereas Tintoretto—"

"One moment. Who's Tintoretto?"

"Just a fancy on my part, Mr. Delphick, it was simply that he made me think of Tintoretto's self-portrait, I'm sure you know it. The beard, you know, and that dreadfully haunted expression."

"Let me be quite clear in my mind about this, please. You saw a man who reminded you of Tintoretto at the tennis match, and it was the same man who crept up behind you last night?"

"As I have just been explaining, Mr. Delphick."

"Yes. Thank you. I'm sorry to sound stupid, but how could you tell, in the dark?"

"Well, I must admit that it didn't occur to me at the time. I was, you see, in a somewhat agitated frame of mind. And for a minute or two immediately after I broke my torch, it seemed like pitch darkness. But one of the men who came out of the vestry was carrying a tiny flashlight, and I suppose I must have unconsciously registered some sort of impression before the one in charge made him switch it off."

"So it didn't occur to you at the time. So may I ask, when did it? Occur to you, I mean. That it was the same man—" Delphick broke off abruptly, appalled to hear himself sounding exactly like Miss Seeton in full cry. Fortunately nobody else seemed to have noticed.

"Some time later. After Dr. Wright and Anne had very kindly put disinfectant on a few little scratches here and there and I was really quite comfortable in bed, not dreaming for a second that dear Bob had volunteered to stay, and was trying to settle down on this quite unsuitable sofa—"

"Yes, yes, we think he'll live, Miss Seeton—"

"Now you're teasing me, Mr. Delphick."

Delphick grinned. "Sorry. Overeager. Take your time."

"Yes, well, all at once I remembered his beard tickling my neck, you see. And then I must have gone to sleep, because I had a rather confused dream, no doubt because I'd been thinking about *Aida*. It *was* Victoria Sladen, by the way, I'm sure of it. But not carrying a tennis racket, that goes without saying. On one of those dreadful foggy nights we used to have every winter in London until they did away with coal fires. In the fifties, wasn't it?"

"Killer smog, they called it," Brinton chipped in, earning himself a glare from Delphick. "Diabolical, it used to be," he added insouciantly.

"And I woke up at some stage in the night, and simply knew that it was Tintoretto."

Delphick pondered, and then looked up hopefully. "You haven't got a reproduction of this painting among your art books, by any chance? It's not essential, I'm sure we can get one from Hatchards or somewhere, but—"

Miss Seeton was shaking her head sadly. "I'm afraid not. I did make a sketch of the man afterwards, if that might be of interest. After the tennis match, that is." She got up and went to rummage through the untidy stacks of sketches on the writing surface of her old-fashioned desk, while her visitors watched her in admiration mixed with awe.

chapter

~11~

"Be reasonable," Mel pleaded, with a luscious smile. Delphick couldn't remember ever having seen her look more seductively feminine. She had waylaid him and Ranger in the George and Dragon, after Chief Inspector Brinton and DC Foxon had gobbled their sandwiches and gone off, Brinton having decided they should both interview the vicars of the other two churches burgled during the night.

"I'm always reasonable, Mel. Sergeant Ranger here will confirm that when I do roar, I roar as gently as any sucking dove." Bob raised his eyes to heaven but judged it better to remain silent. "But when I say no comment, I mean no comment."

Delphick liked and respected Amelita Forby. Often enough in the past she had proved herself to be a valued ally, and he had no wish to alienate her. On the other hand, he had a lot of thinking to do before deciding how best to act on the startling information Miss Seeton had so nonchalantly provided. He certainly wasn't anything like ready to allow himself to be quoted in the tabloid press.

"But everybody in Plummergen's talking about it, for heaven's sake. Don't you realize how efficient the gossip grapevine is in a village? They've all heard about the burglaries at the other two churches as well. And above all, there are all kinds of wild stories going round about Miss Seeton. Listen, if you think you're going to be able to keep her name out of the papers, you're off your rocker. As a matter of fact, I'm going to give this to the *Sunday Negative*. There's just time. If I wait for my usual spot in Monday's *Daily*, other people'll probably have picked it up and the competition might run spoilers."

"*Tomorrow's* paper? Out of the question. In any case, this whole thing's a matter for the Kent County Constabulary, not Scotland Yard," Delphick said, wincing inwardly as he heard himself being pompous. "Mr. Brinton may have something to say to the media after he's visited the other two villages concerned."

"Oh, foo nuts to that!" Mel felt simply marvelous. Wow, who needs sleep, anyway? She reckoned her strength was as the strength of ten all right, but not, as the Scriptures had it, because her heart was pure. Oh dear no, quite the reverse. She could *just* bear to be apart from scrumptious Thrudd for an hour or so while he was out taking pictures of the church, the vicar, and with any luck Miss S. herself, but had plans for the two of them after she'd phoned her story through to the news desk of the *Negative's* Sunday edition.

"Let me tell you something," she went on after gulping and doing her best to banish the more distracting mental images of pleasures to come to the back burner of her consciousness. "My paper isn't paying me to sit here in Plummergen and let the *Kent Messenger* or *Brettenden Advertiser* or some other local rag send some pimply youth along to talk to Brinton and scoop this story. Here, I don't know why I'm so nice to you, but you can read what I've drafted."

Mel rootled in her shoulder bag and took out a spiral-bound note pad. It was already open, and she flipped back a couple of pages before handing it to Delphick. "Don't worry, it isn't shorthand. And at school I once got a prize for Legible Handwriting."

This is what Delphick read:

VERSATILE BATTLING BROLLY SWOPS WEAPONS

Warm Reception For Thieves In The Night

The villagers of sleepy Plummergen in Kent are justly proud of their local celebrity, retired art teacher Emily Seeton (writes Amelita Forby, our prize-winning Seeton-watcher). Loyal *Negative* readers will recall many of the redoubtable little lady's exploits during recent years, and will be thrilled to learn that she has within the last day or two shown that she's in her usual sparkling form.

This unlikely scourge of the criminal fraternity is rarely parted from the trusty umbrella that has featured in so many of her notable adventures. But when she popped into the village church late on Friday evening to plan her flower arrangements for the forthcoming Sunday services, even Miss Seeton reckoned she could do without it. She carried instead a long and hefty flashlight of the kind sensible country folk keep handy.

Which was lucky for her and unlucky for the trio of burglars she surprised in the act of cleaning out the cupboard containing the church's treasured collection of silver chalices and other rare items. Wielding her flashlight like King Arthur's legendary sword Excalibur, Miss Seeton waded into the crooks and gave them a thoroughly disagreeable quarter of an hour before they fled in panic, but alas with their loot intact. It later emerged that two other village churches in the area were similarly burgled during Friday night, and

Kent police are assuming that the same gang was responsible, getting away with a total haul worth many thousands of pounds.

Interviewed on the day after her ordeal, demure but spry Miss Seeton coolly insisted to your reporter that she had done, "nothing out of the ordinary" and that the whole episode was "all most unfortunate." Asked if she hadn't been a little rash in having a go in the face of odds of three determined crooks against one retired lady teacher, Miss Seeton smiled inscrutably.

It seems it was all in the day's—or rather, night's—work for Scotland Yard's part-time consultant and favorite senior citizen, of whom on hearing the news the Yard's Chief Superintendent Delphick said, "Blah blah blah, and moreover blah. Miss Seeton has already provided the police with valuable information, which is expected to lead to early arrests. Blah blah."

Having read the piece not once but twice, Delphick sighed, shaking his head from side to side slowly, and passed the pad to Ranger. Then he gazed at Mel, a lugubrious expression on his face. "I congratulate you," he said. "You have a flawless command of the *Negative's* appalling house style, and a splendidly cavalier attitude to the facts. That's not what happened at all, and you know it."

Mel shrugged. "First rule of popular journalism: don't let the facts get in the way of a good story."

"Please, Mel. I know it's not exactly a state secret that Miss S. does some work for us, but do you *have* to spell it out like that? And I absolutely refuse to be quoted. Blah blah indeed!"

"You get to fill in the blahs, Mr. Delphick. They're just to indicate the rough length of quote I want from you."

"No, no, a thousand times no."

"Oh dear. Well, in that case I guess I shall just have to fill up the space by mentioning that quite coincidentally, there's another newsworthy person in Plummergen at the moment, a star tennis player staying incognito as a house-guest at the home of the local squire, Sir George Colveden. Won't I? That should bring the Fleet Street rat pack here in double quick time." Mel batted her eyelids languorously.

"Mel, you *wouldn't*!" Then, after an moment or two, "Would you?"

"Try me."

"How the blazes did you find out, anyway?" Delphick wheeled round in his chair and glared at Ranger. "Is this your doing? If it is, may the Lord have mercy on you, for I certainly won't."

"Calm down, Mr. Delphick. Of course it wasn't Bob." Mel sighed. "Honestly, you high-up officials can be so naive. You cook up your little secret schemes and imagine the rest of us are too dumb to put two and two together. Why in the world do you suppose a couple of high-priced journos like Thrudd and me just happen to be lurking around Plummergen? Simply on the off-chance that Miss S. is about to perform one of her conjuring tricks? Mind you, it's a pretty safe bet that *something* weird'll happen to her in any average week, but face it, this burglary deal's not much of a story. It wouldn't rate two column inches in the nationals if she hadn't already been notorious. No sirree, I was on to the Trish Thumper affair from the word go, and we're here to watch what Miss S. makes of it when she gets involved. As I'll bet my bottom dollar she will."

"My apologies, Bob. It was unworthy of me to entertain even for a moment the idea that you might have blabbed. I should have realized that this ruthless female would outwit me yet again. And now you see her holding me to ransom."

"Oh, come on. It isn't that bad. Give me my notebook

back, Bob. Let's have another look at that last para.'' Mel considered it. ''I'll offer you a deal, okay? Keep me in the picture, and I won't breathe a word about you know who until you give me the go-ahead. And I'll cut the part-time consultant reference and make that last para read . . . 'all in the day's work, etcetera, for this amazing lady whose reputation is as high among senior police officers as it is among readers of the *Negative*. Told of the news, Scotland Yard's Chief Superintendent Delphick said, ''We have good reason to be grateful to Miss Seeton for her public-spirited actions in the past, and I am not at all surprised to hear that she has once again demonstrated her bravery and resourcefulness.'' ' Okay?''

Delphick thought about it for a while. It was horribly risky to trust a determined, highly professional newspaperwoman like Mel. Then he remembered the times he had done so previously—and the fact that this time he had no option in the matter anyway—and nodded. ''Okay, you win. And, er, by the way, you can leave in the last bit about her having provided useful information likely to lead to early arrests.''

''You sure?''

''Yes. She has done, actually, and seeing it in print might scare somebody into doing something silly.''

''Now then,'' Norman said sharply over the telephone, ''I don't want you doin' nothin' silly. I know you've 'ad your troubles with the fuzz, but you don't know 'em like I do.'' He listened quietly enough while William Parsons replied at some length. ''Not a bit of it,'' he said then. ''I saw the paper an hour ago. 'Ad longer to think about it than what you 'ave. An' I already woke up 'Arvey out of 'is beauty sleep an' told 'im. Right, I'll admit it's a bit of a facer that old girl turnin' out to be 'oo she is, but it don't change nothin', Bill. All that about an early arrest, dear oh dear, they always put out that sort o' guff, just to kid their guv'nors they're earnin' their pay. Woss that? Lie low? Not on your nelly, my lad. Nah, a deal's a deal. We know where Thumper's kid is, an' me 'n' Arvey'll do our bit. Fact is, I'm nippin' back down that way meself later on, when the pubs are open. Loose lot o' tongues them rustics've got. I'll give you another bell tonight, when I've worked out ways an' means. Meantime, cheer up, cully, we in't dead yet, not even breathin' 'eavy.''

After he had replaced the receiver, Norman sucked his teeth for a while and then picked it up again and dialed another number. The ringing tone seemed to go on for quite a long time, but eventually there was a response.

''About flippin' time. S'me again. What? In the bath? You know what, you overdo them baths o' yours, you'll dry up all yer natural oils. A feller in a pub told me that 'appened to 'is ol' lady. Listen, 'Arve. Remember what I told yer after Bill went 'ome that night? About 'is barmy idea o' snatchin' that bird? Well, we might be lendin' 'im an 'and.'' He held out the receiver at arm's length until the agitated quacking sound emerging from the earpiece died down, then spoke again.

''You're beginnin' to repeat yerself, son. Pin back yer lug'ole an' listen. Like I said, I'm the only one what said a dicky bird in that church. You got no cause to get into a mucksweat. Any'ow, I still don't reckon there's a snowball's chance in 'ell she got a make on any of us. On the other 'and, they do say she's a fly ol' soul, so I bin workin' out ways an' means o' takin' out a bit of what yer might call insurance. Nah, not over the blower. Meet me tomorrer mornin', my place, arpass ten.''

• • •

"Thrudd, darling?"

"Mmm?"

"It's morning, you gorgeous creature."

"Don't wanna know."

"Sunday. So we can always come back to bed later, but you'd better go back to your own room before the maid comes round to do the beds. The coast'll be clear again by the time we've had breakfast and popped out to get the *Negative*."

"Screw the maid."

Mel gazed down at him proudly. "You couldn't possibly," she murmured. "Not even you, superman. Not after . . . oh, and by the way, don't try to raise the roller blind."

"Roller blind? Whaddya mean?"

"I have a feeling you might go up with it."

Lady Colveden entered the kitchen and stopped short in astonishment. "Why are you brandishing that rose, Nigel?"

"Rose? What rose? Oh, you mean this rose."

"Yes. The one you're brandishing."

"Hardly *brandishing*, I should have thought, Ma. I say, you're up jolly early, aren't you?"

"Don't evade the question. Nigel, there is a tray on the table."

"Oh. So there is."

"And on it, a pot of tea, jug of milk, etcetera. And two of my special Fortnum's biscuits on a plate."

"Absolutely."

"Very well. Place the rose beside the plate, and I shall then carry her early morning tea up to Patricia in her room."

"Oh. Well, actually, I had—"

"I can see perfectly well what you had in mind, Nigel. Quite apart from the fact that you've shaved already and reek of cologne." Her mouth twitched. "Sorry, dear, but

I have to explain that women of any age past puberty prefer not to receive gentlemen callers until they've looked at themselves in the mirror, shrieked inwardly, and then done something about what they saw. Cheer up, I'll tell her the rose is from you."

Halfway through the door, Meg Colveden looked back, suddenly aghast. "Nigel—you haven't been doing this every morning since she arrived, have you?"

"No," said Nigel despondently. "Only occurred to me first thing today."

"Well, thank heavens for that." She took pity on the son she adored. "Tell you what, it's Sunday, so no practice session today, right? Why don't you invite Patricia to go out for a stroll with you later on? Sharpen your appetites for lunch. I'm sure she'll say yes."

Nigel's face brightened. "Do you really think so, Ma?"

"Of course she will."

Because I shall make it crystal clear to her that she'd bloody well better, Lady Colveden said to herself as she mounted the stairs with the tray.

Norah Blaine heard Erica Nuttel return to the house. The way she banged the door behind her would have wakened the dead, but Norah was in any case up and about. She hastily popped their eggs into the water she had already brought to the boil, and set the timer at four minutes. Eric was inclined to be fussy about her egg. Turning to her friend when she entered the kitchen, Norah glanced in puzzlement at the folded newspaper under her arm.

"Why have you been out to buy a paper, Eric? The boy delivered our *Sunday Telegraph* ages ago. Oh dear, you do look cross."

"I am not in the least cross," Miss Nuttel said, but Mrs. Blaine knew she was. She had over their years together become something of a connoisseur of her friends's moods. "Nor am I surprised, for I quite expected something of the kind. I am, however, disgusted. Look for yourself."

Mrs. Blaine took the paper thrust toward her and unfolded it. It was already open at page three, which was dominated by the headline BRITAIN IS PROUD OF YOU, MISS S.! Subeditors cherish the privilege of inventing their own titles, but the report Mrs. Blaine read was substantially as Mel Forby had dictated it over the telephone the previous afternoon.

"Oh dear, the eggs are ready." Mrs. Blaine said as the timer buzzed. She took the saucepan off the stove, spooned the eggs into bright red china egg cups embellished with Tweetie-pie cartoons, put them on the table, and then sank weakly into a chair.

"And is that all you have to say for yourself, pray?"

"Well, I can see that you must find it very upsetting, Eric."

"Upsetting? It's preposterous! It is perfectly obvious to me that once more a complete perversion of justice is taking place. The Forby creature and That Woman were themselves behind those burglaries, Norah. It's clear to me now that they were plotting the details that afternoon. Why else would That Woman have been in the church at night? Planning flower arrangements indeed! In the dark? No, she supervised the whole thing, saw her criminal associates safely off the premises, and then claimed to have tried to stop them. And now this Forby has duly printed the farrago of lies they prepared between them in advance."

"When you put it like that, Erica—"

"Even you can see the force of my argument. Precisely."

"But what are you going to do?"

"My duty."

"What, you mean go to the police?"

"Really, Norah! What on earth would be the point of

that? The police are in her pocket. No, I intend to denounce her publicly.''

''When you did that at the Women's Institute, they wouldn't listen. Said we hadn't paid our subs.''

''I shall choose my time and place, Norah. Now eat your egg before it gets cold.''

chapter
~12~

CHIEF SUPERINTENDENT Delphick sat in his office at New Scotland Yard musing on the difficulties of getting anything done on a Sunday. It had been a good many years since he had been liable to be rostered for weekend duty in the ordinary way, and the occasions he *had* been called out on the Sabbath had for the most part required his presence at the scene of some spectacular crime or emergency, with appropriate specialists in busy attendance, weekend or no weekend. He had therefore fallen into the habit of assuming that, just as the metropolitan police force seemed to carry on as usual when he was away on his annual vacations, so it did on Saturdays and Sundays. He couldn't remember when he had last entered his own office other than on a weekday, and it had come as a shock to him that day to discover that it was like a blessed tomb.

So far as that went, so was much of the rest of the building. The few people about looked as if they had no business to be there, so oddly attired were they. Faces belonging to people he knew to be staid, conventionally minded functionaries in normal circumstances now appeared above sporty ensembles. The one person he had found in the press and PR department—a young woman in a sleeveless cotton blouse, abbreviated skirt, and sandals on otherwise bare feet—had chatted with slightly flirtatious informality to him for several minutes before he recognized her as the normally subdued and earnest Miss Moody of Handouts & Cuttings.

Miss Moody had at least been through the papers by the time Delphick turned up, and confirmed that none of the rival Sundays had been in time to pick up the *Negative*'s story. It was by no means to be taken for granted that the Plummergen burglars read the *Negative*: one simply had to hope that they did.

At all events, a few phone calls had made it pretty clear that it was going to be a miracle if Delphick managed to get anywhere at all that day in his attempt to identify the man depicted in two of the three sketches now lying before him on the top of his desk. Miss Seeton had, as always, been shy about showing them and reluctant to hand them over, even when reminded that it was for her services as an artist that she was paid a retainer by Scotland Yard.

Delphick pulled a face and scribbled a note on the pad beside him to remind him to have another word with the finance people. It seemed the blasted computer was *still* making out her checks to MISSESS instead of Emily D. Seeton. Even though the manager of the Brettenden branch of her bank had at last grasped the nature of the problem, he was insisting that Miss Seeton endorsed them to herself with the countersignature which, she protested mildly, made her feel furtive and even slightly dishonest.

Bless her, she continued to be worth every penny of the modest fees that, added to her small schoolteacher's pension, enabled Miss Seeton to sustain her unpretentious style of life in Plummergen. Delphick smiled to himself, wondering for the umpteenth time how it came about that this mild, unassertive person managed with such consistency to find herself at the center of startling, indeed violent, events. A human lightning rod, Sir Hubert Everleigh liked to say—liking it so much indeed that he was inclined to make the point several times whenever Miss Seeton's name came up in discussion—frequently producing not electrical but criminal charges. However dubious the physics implied in Sir Heavily's analogy, Delphick saw his point.

Miss Seeton might be in many ways the very model of the gentle spinster living in quiet retirement, but there weren't many dull moments when she was around. And the things that happened in her vicinity fed what was certainly one hell of an imagination. This drawing on top, for example. If she'd chosen to go in for political cartooning instead of teaching art to schoolgirls, Miss S. could have been another Vicky. With a few dashing strokes of her stick of charcoal she'd evoked an astonishingly vivid likeness of Sir Wilfred Thumper. A Thumper in what might or might not have been judicial robes, but wearing on his head not a conventional judge's wig, but a sort of tight-fitting nightcap. Whatever it was, it concealed his ears and had the effect of focusing attention on the thin lips, clenched jaw and deeply lined face. The face of a fanatic, Delphick decided as he studied it, capable of inflicting appalling cruelty in the name of some high-sounding principle.

Or was it? Wasn't it rather that of a disillusioned, sarcastic schoolmaster, a clever man wondering how on earth the high promise his university teachers had claimed to discern in him had melted away, leaving him despising himself as a hack, poorly paid to try to drum some sensitivity into a pack of spotty, yobbish yahoos?

It was something about the smallish but dreamy eyes, deep-set in that bony face, that momentarily made Delphick feel sorry for the subject of Miss Seeton's picture, and remember his own contradictory reactions to the man when he had called on him. The eyes, and the fact that Miss Seeton had depicted him grasping the hand of a little girl, about five or six years of age but clearly recognizable as his daughter Patricia, and equally obviously trying to tug herself free. No prizes for interpreting that one, Delphick thought, and set it on one side to look yet again at the second sketch.

So this was the mystery man: the chap in the St. John's Ambulance Brigade uniform who had caught Miss Seeton's eye at the Hurlingham Club that afternoon. The same man, she insisted, who had taken her by surprise from behind in Plummergen church and on whom she had inflicted if not grievous bodily harm then at least minor injuries with the business end of a long and heavy flashlight. It was probably only the filament of the bulb that had been broken in the struggle, and Miss Seeton would get her torch back in working order again in the fullness of time.

Good for Thrudd Banner: not everyone would have shown his presence of mind. After he and Mel had come to Miss Seeton's aid, untied her and got her home, Banner had gone back to the church with two clean plastic food bags. Wearing one over one hand, he had gingerly picked up the torch by one end from the stone floor of the nave and popped it into the other in order to preserve any evidence it might bear. With a bit of luck her assailant had made a grab at it and left a print, or Miss S. might even have broken the perisher's skin: no blood was visible to the naked eye but you never knew what the forensic boffins might come up with, and a blood group identification was a lot better than nothing.

Extraordinary-looking chap, this Tintoretto character, in Miss S.'s version, anyhow. One might as well call him that for want of a better name. Talk about Thumper's eyes: this fellow's were like nothing so much as shadowed pools of despair. Delphick was rather taken by the felicity of his phrase and repeated it to himself aloud. Or perhaps the eyes of a St. Bernard dog after a long day carting his little barrel of brandy up and down Alpine passes. Heavy lids, great bags underneath, glazed expression, generally a sense of exhaustion, but fundamentally kindly all the same. Hardly the sort of eyes you'd expect to belong to the kind of thug capable of jumping a frail—well, frail-*looking*—elderly lady in the dark.

The St. Bernard image wasn't a bad one, actually, because this Tintoretto character had a big, squishy sort of nose and a droopy mouth. You couldn't see any dewlaps, on account of all the whiskers, but dewlaps there might very possibly be lurking behind them. Just standing there in some sort of black uniform, like death warmed up. Memo, do they let the inmates grow beards in jug these days? Probably, England's been a hairy sort of place for the past ten years or so, especially since the Beatles & Co started throwing their money at all those unhygienic-looking Indian gurus.

Have to find out, all the same. Miss S. might have made Tintoretto's whiskers a bit more exuberant than they were in real life, but they looked like a long-term project. And they'd been thinking in terms of an ex-con who was only released a matter of months ago, well, less than a year, anyway. Could ring up the Royal Navy, perhaps, ask them how long they reckon it takes a man to grow a full set.

Another memo, to add to the others. Delphick could see he was going to be spending a fair old time on the phone the next day, one way and another. Secretary of the Hurlingham Club, to find out what they did about first-aid cover at important events attracting a lot of spectators. The idiot who'd answered the phone half an hour earlier had been utterly useless. Probably some relief barman just hired for the day.

Then he'd have to make a call to St. John's Ambulance

Brigade HQ tomorrow, when their office was manned. One easy question and one hard one for them: which local branch, chapter or whatever they called it would be responsible for fielding volunteers to be in attendance at the Hurlingham Club, and did they perchance maintain a national register of the names of people who'd been members during the past, say, ten years?

Copies of Criminal Records Office's mug shots of all the people on Delphick's list of possibles would, he'd been promised, be on his desk first thing Monday morning. That probably meant around lunch time. He had quite enough faith in Miss Seeton's skill to be confident that if Chummy *was* one of those possibles, he'd be able to make a match by then, but surely there was *something* that could be done to move things along a bit in the meantime.

The National Gallery was open on a Sunday afternoon. Pop in and have a squint at the paintings Miss S. had mentioned? Wait a minute, though, had she said all three of them were in the National? Bellini's doge, definitely. Not too sure about Tintoretto. No matter, easy enough to get hold of one of those coffee-table collections of reproductions. No need to trek all the way to Hatchard's. They'd probably have one in the book department at the Army & Navy Stores just across the road in Victoria Street, or even the Great Smith Street public library. And the third one, what was that name she'd mentioned?

Delphick turned to the third drawing, the weirdest of the lot, and searched his memory. Titian, that was it, and something about death. Got it, The Death of Actaeon. In the National Gallery. And there, in Miss Seeton's version, was Trish Thumper yet again, a definitely adult Trish with her right boob hanging out of her tennis dress, lunging forward waving her tennis racket, egging on a pack of hounds. Two of them had already reached and were leaping up to drag down and savage their quarry, which was—good heavens, it was so subtly suggested and deeply shaded that one hadn't made it out earlier—surely it was miserable old Tintoretto again? And the faces of those two hounds baying for his blood, could they possibly bear a hint of resemblance to those of Wilfred Thumper and, and *himself*? He looked more closely, held the drawing up so that the light from the window fell directly on it, and thought about it hard. They did, by crikey, and that was a bit much, even for Miss S.!

Delphick sat up straight and pulled himself together. When Miss Seeton's subconscious or unconscious, mystical third eye or prophetic gift or whatever it was directed her hand, it didn't pay to allow oneself to feel insulted by the message. If one of those dogs did look a bit like him and Tintoretto was the quarry, well, fair enough. He and Thumper *were* after blood, metaphorically speaking, anyway.

Not necessarily Tintoretto's, of course. One had to keep a clear head about that. Miss S. was convinced that Tintoretto was one of the three men who'd made off with the Plummergen church silver. That was a criminal offense of course, but hardly one for the Yard. Chris Brinton was perfectly capable of dealing with it. Miss S. definitely hadn't *said* a word to suggest that she thought the fellow had anything to do with the Thumper blackmailing affair.

On the other hand, and knowing why Trish was staying with the Colvedens, she'd drawn a picture suggesting the clearest possible link. Pointed the finger, or rather the tennis racket, directly at Tintoretto as being someone better out of the way from Trish's point of view.

When they did finally manage to put a proper name to this chap and run him and his associates to earth, he was in any case going to have a lot of explaining to do. Even after Brinton had got them bang to rights on the burglary and assault charges. Tintoretto might flatly deny having been at the Hurlingham Club, but Miss Seeton's word would be worth a lot more than his if it came to that.

In any case, there were probably plenty of photographs of the Trish Thumper *vs* Nancy Wiesendonck match knocking about waiting to be turned up if necessary. Assuming the mystery man was there got up as a first-aider, he would have been ideally placed to lace Trish's drink with something to give her the collywobbles and put her off her game. He would also have had a ringside view of her discomfiture and had time to write that last anonymous letter to her father and drop it in a letter box outside the club, thus accounting for the postmark on the envelope.

In short, the case of Regina v. Tintoretto might not be completely watertight just yet, but it was coming along nicely; even if it didn't make much sense for a blackmailer with a lot on his mind to go in for a spot of burglary on the side. Especially when he did it on Miss Emily D. Seeton's home patch, as Delphick hoped he and his accomplices had discovered by this time.

He stood up and stretched, took a last look at all three drawings, and then carefully locked them away. They'd have to be photocopied, of course, and copies could be shown to the assistant commissioner the next day. Sir Heavily was a great fan of Miss Seeton's and perfectly capable of nabbing the originals for his private collection given half the chance.

chapter

–13–

IN ORDER to make his return visit to Plummergen, Norman Proctor borrowed the ancient and battered van belonging to his landlord and friend Charlie Yung Fat. Charlie lived in the house next door, where he presided over a household consisting, in addition to himself, of a silent wife, a wizened mother, and numerous children, the eldest of whom, Verity, worked in the city, was studying hard for her accountancy exams, and could therefore help out in the Jade Garden only now and again in the evenings. The others had no similar excuse not to rally round.

Considering all the unpaid pairs of hands he had at his disposal and the popularity of the restaurant, Norman reckoned Charlie could have afforded a really classy set of wheels, a Roller even, but it was the van or nothing. For Charlie was too busy running the business seven days a week to bother his head with thoughts of recreational motoring. He went with one of his sons in the van every weekday morning to pick up his supplies from the wholesale markets and the Loon Fung Chinese supermarket in Chinatown, but was happy enough to lend it to Norman at any other time, provided only that it was always returned with a full tank of petrol.

Not that Norman often availed himself of the privilege. Its customary cargoes of pork, chickens and ducks, dried fish, mysterious sausages, vegetables, desiccated mushrooms, noodles, spices, and pickles had over the years endowed the van with a memorably penetrating aroma. Not to put too fine a point on it, you could smell it from five yards away, and it took real strength of character to get inside and drive it, even with the windows wide open.

It was therefore with a sense of relief that Charlie parked it that Sunday lunchtime in a lay-by just outside Plummergen, withdrew out of range, and sucked in a few refreshing lungfuls of good Kentish air. From his and Harvey's previous researches in the bar of the George and Dragon, he had gained a rough idea of the location of Rytham Hall in relation to the village, and having brought with him the map they had studied while preparing to pillage the churches of the neighborhood, he knew that he was now not far away from the house, which lay ahead and to his left.

What he didn't know was that Trish Thumper, looking forward to her lunch, was striding through the meadow on the other side of the tall hedge beside which he was standing, with a breathless but blissfully happy Nigel Colveden in her wake.

It had been a surprisingly successful outing. Nigel had no idea that Trish's ready acceptance of his timid post-breakfast suggestion that they might go for a stroll had anything to do with his mother's formidable powers of persuasion. Notwithstanding her father's strenuous attempts to keep her in the dark, Trish had worked out for herself with remarkable accuracy the real reasons why she had been invited to stay with the Colvedens. She was grateful to Meg Colveden for making her so welcome, and Sir George's bluff, uncomplicated kindliness and the way he urged second helpings on her at every meal had endeared him to her. She thought Nigel was a bit wet but not bad-looking, and had been quite touched when her hostess explained the presence of the rose, its leaves partially consumed by blackfly, on the tea tray. So why not go for a walk with him if he was so keen on the idea?

They had therefore set off, Trish magnificent in white cotton trousers and a short-sleeved green sports shirt that more or less matched the short green rubber Wellington boots into which the said trousers were tucked. Nigel had been thinking less in terms of a cross-country hike than a gentle saunter down leafy lanes, possibly after a while, and with a lot of luck, hand in hand. On noticing the green wellies he had hurriedly dug up a comfortable old pair of boots of his own to substitute for the casual loafers he had been wearing.

For the first half-hour the conversation had been both desultory and banal. Desultory because once they were out of Rytham Hall grounds and into the rough woodland that lay behind, Trish set such a cracking pace that it was all Nigel could do to catch her up from time to time, come alongside, and force out a few breathless pleasantries before falling back again. Banal because Trish for her part would on the whole have much preferred to have gone for a brisk walk with somebody really interesting like Virginia Wade, and at first made little conversational effort.

Eventually however they came out into open farmland through which a signposted footpath ran. Nigel was able to keep up without getting out of breath, and it dawned on Trish that she wasn't being very kind to the young man who was, after all, cheerfully giving up a great deal of his time to ferrying her back and forth between Rytham Hall and the practice courts, while pretending not to notice they were being followed by a carload of coppers. He was after all really a pretty decent chap, as well as being the son and heir of a well-to-do baronet. Trish wasn't familiar with the phrase *chevalier sans peur et sans reproche*, but if she had been, that is very probably how she would at that moment have summed up Nigel Colveden.

So when they came to a stile and Nigel courteously and quite unnecessarily helped her over it, Trish allowed him briefly to retain possession of her hand, read the mute appeal in his eyes, and then in a businesslike fashion took him into her powerful arms and kissed him lengthily and thoroughly. Crushed against that Amazonian bosom and enveloped by the fragrance of Camay bath soap, Nigel in a blaze of intuition decided that the Prophet had been absolutely on the right lines when he drew up the specifications for the Moslem Paradise.

"You're really quite sweet, you know," Trish then said, to the lush sound of massed violins as supplied by Nigel's imagination. "But don't stand there like that. You've gone sort of cross-eyed. Come on, we ought to be heading for the house if we're going to be back in time for lunch."

Compared with the exquisite poetry of the first four words, the remainder of what she said struck Nigel as being a shade disappointing, and the sound of the violins diminished accordingly. Nigel was all in favor of her going into quite a bit more detail about his sweetness, and then his taking over for a while with a rapturous monologue on the subject of Trish's radiant beauty, exquisitely sensitive and generous nature, and his own unworthiness. Then, after a few reruns of that incredible kiss, he thought he might venture some remarks on the theme of the undesirability of long engagements.

It was not to be. For some reason Trish seemed to view their embrace as being less than earth-shattering, and to be disinclined to pursue the conversation along the above lines.

She was otherwise agreeable enough, though, speaking warmly of the comforts of Rytham Hall and a touch wistfully of Nigel's good fortune in having been landed with a couple of very satisfactory parents.

"Ma's all right," he admitted. "And I suppose Dad means well, even if he is barking mad."

"He is nothing of the kind, Nigel Colveden. He's a cuddly old poppet and don't you forget it."

"*Dad?* Cuddly? Good grief!"

"Distinctly cuddly. And I know what I'm talking about, because I'm stuck with this horrendous sourpuss of a father who chews nails for breakfast. His idea of a relaxing read is probably Fox's *Book Of Martyrs*. Mind you, I expect he reckons most of them got off much too lightly."

"I say, Trish, would you say I was, um, as cuddly as Dad?"

Trish stopped, turned, and surveyed him. "Couldn't say, I've never tried your father, but I doubt it. You're *reasonably* cuddly, I must admit. Oh, all right then. One more, and then straight back to the house. Come here."

Thus it was that Nigel was again rubbery-kneed and blissfully happy during the last part of their walk, that even Trish was more than just healthily pink about the cheeks, and that the two young people were amicably wrangling about Sir Wilfred Thumper when they came into earshot of Norman on the other side of the hedge.

". . . and what's more, my father's the stingiest man I've ever known. I'm not surprised people can't stand him."

"Come off it, Trish. Sir W. Thumper may be a lot of things, but at least you can't claim he's stingy. Dash it, he's treating us all to seats at Glyndebourne the day after tomorrow. You, me, and my aged parents. Plus himself and your mother. That's going to set him back a packet."

"Ha! Bet you anything Mummy's paid. And even if by some remote chance he did cough up, if I know him, he'll charge it up to official expenses . . . Nigel, can you smell anything?"

"Only you, darling Trish." Fervently.

"No, hands off, you horror. I'm being serious."

"So am I."

"Something like won-ton soup, or maybe fried crispy noodles. Whatever can it be?"

"You're imagining things. Ma's Sunday lunches are pretty good, but hardly what you'd call exotic . . ."

The sound of their voices faded into the distance, but Norman made no attempt to keep in range. He had heard enough to enable him to conceive a brilliant idea.

Miss Seeton always looked forward to her visits to Rytham Hall, and unless the weather was bad enjoyed walking there. Dear Lady Colveden, thoughtful as ever, had telephoned that morning to suggest that if she were still feeling the effects of her ordeal in the church Sir George would be delighted to fetch her in the big car, but the bruises were more colorful than painful, and what better therapy could there be in any case than the gentle exercise involved in a twenty-minute walk?

How kind the Colvedens always were, and how generous their hospitality at the hall. An interesting word, hospitality, its meaning so much closer to the original Latin than that suggested, nowadays at least, by the word hospital. *Hospes*, that is. A guest. Being woken up too early and made to do raffia work when not very well hardly makes one feel like a guest. Especially when one has had to pay.

The orders of Knights Hospitallers wouldn't have charged for their services, of course. And a baronet was after all simply a superior, hereditary kind of knight, so Sir George, so free with his invitations, was a modern hospitaller. Well, perhaps not exactly superior. Hadn't King James I invented baronetcies and sold them to raise money? Like the scandal involving Lloyd George and that man Maundy Gregory in one's own young days.

By the time she had reached the outskirts of Plummergen, Miss Seeton's thoughts had drifted on through Maundy Gregory the honors broker to the "maundy money" presented on Maundy Thursday by the sovereign to as many old men and women as there were years of her age. That made her think of almshouses, and in no time she was back to hospitals and knights hospitaller, and of course, the St. John's Ambulance Brigade was an offshoot of just such an order!

Miss Seeton blinked a few times, looked about her, and realized that she had walked most of the way to Rytham Hall without noticing the fact. Yes, the gates to the driveway were just a hundred yards or so beyond the van parked at the side of the road with its bonnet propped open and the gentleman leaning over the engine. Oh dear. Much as one wanted to be helpful whenever possible, mechanical problems were something best left to those who understood them. It cost nothing to be polite to a stranger encountered on the highway, however.

"Good morning! Or should it be good afternoon? One is never quite sure after twelve noon but before lunch, is one?"

Being occupied in cursing Charlie Yung Fat for allowing his van's radiator to have run dry, Norman had not heard Miss Seeton approach. Startled by her voice, he straightened up so suddenly that his head came into collision with the underside of the open bonnet and dislodged the metal rod that held it up. When he told Harvey later that it bloomin' nearly decapitated him, Norman was not being quite truthful, but he undoubtedly sustained a painful blow to the nape of his neck and at the same time blistered the palms of his hands on the still very hot radiator as he scrabbled, moaning incoherently, to free himself.

He then suffered the further shock of realizing that he had seen the elderly lady now standing beside him with an expression of great concern on her face before. Struggling to free herself from William Parsons. Just for a moment, by the dim light of Harvey's pen-torch. And that he had left her trussed up on the floor of the nave of Plummergen church, having addressed her at some length with no attempt to disguise his voice. And finally that she was no less a person than Miss Emily D. Seeton, the Battling Brolly.

Norman had always prided himself on his quick thinking when in tight corners, but he had never previously crammed such intensive mental exercise into a mere second or two. He hadn't disguised his voice then, so he'd have to do it now, while seeing double as a result of that wallop on the bonce, keeping out of range of that blasted brolly she was holding, and trying to disregard the pain in his hands.

"Oh my goodness, you poor man! That must have been extremely painful."

Swaying on his feet, Norman somehow managed to summon up what he imagined was a nonchalant smile but was in fact a ghastly grimace. "Aio naio, nawt a tawl," he fluted. "Ay mainor mishawp."

"Has your, ah, vehicle broken down? I fear that I have no understanding—"

"Naio, nawt brayken dawn. Naio wottah in the rawdiawtah."

By watching his lips rather than attempting to recognize the weird sounds that issued from them, Miss Seeton managed to grasp the gist of what the man was saying. "Water? You require water? Nothing could be simpler. Rytham Hall is just along here, and I am on my way there for luncheon.

If you will come with me I am quite sure the Colvedens will be delighted to provide you with as much water as you need. Oh dear, you do look a little shaky, perhaps you would care to use this as a walking stick? Here—'' Offering him her umbrella, Miss Seeton was surprised when Norman reared away from it wildly, caught his trouser leg on the end of the front fender, and fell headlong onto the grass verge.

''Ai'm quaite all rate,'' he insisted when he had dragged himself up onto all fours; but Miss Seeton shook her head firmly.

''I have a better idea. You stay here, and I will go to the hall and ask Nigel to bring the water and help you. It shouldn't take more than ten minutes. And some vaseline or something for your hands.''

Norman gazed up at her and feebly nodded agreement. Then, after she had turned and started to march purposefully toward Rytham Hall, he slumped back onto the grass and swore long and eloquently.

''You were right you know, Trish,'' Nigel said when he returned to the house some twenty minutes later, just in time to join the others at the table.

''What about?''

''You remember you thought you could smell Chinese food? Well, you did. That van reeked of it. Terrible old banger, but we got it started all right once I'd filled up the rad. Peculiar chap, wasn't he, Miss Seeton? You know, it beats me how you made head or tail of what he was saying. Talked as though he had a mouth full of marbles or something. Wonder who he was?''

''Chinaman, was he? Good Lord, they seem to be all over the place these days. Like those Indian wallahs that are buying up all the grocery shops—''

Allowing the others to try to put Sir George back on the right lines, Miss Seeton demurely concentrated on Lady Colveden's excellent salmon mousse and kept her own counsel.

chapter

–14–

"I SEE. At least, I think I do. But as through a glass, darkly. Who was it put it like that?"

"St. Paul, I fancy, sir."

"You always know, confound it! Sometimes you sound for all the world like Jeeves."

Delphick thought for a moment, decided to feel flattered, and grinned. "We endeavor to give satisfaction, sir," he intoned in a Jeevesish voice.

Sir Hubert Everleigh stood up, pottered over to the coat-rack in the corner near the door of his office, and took up the old putter he kept there. Addressing an imaginary golf ball, he kept his head down and wiggled his wrists, carrying on the conversation as he did so.

"All this was on Saturday, though, and Amelita Forby's piece duly appeared in yesterday's *Negative*. Any reactions to that, by the way?"

"Possibly. Sergeant Ranger rang me from Plummergen this morning, to pass on something young Nigel Colveden mentioned when they happened to meet yesterday evening. It seems there was a suspicious character hanging about in the vicinity of Rytham Hall earlier that day, around lunch-time. With an old wreck of a van, apparently broken down.

Miss Seeton was on her way to lunch with the Colvedens, so she encountered the man first. He said his radiator had run dry, so she told him to stay put, went on to the hall, and explained the situation to Nigel, who took a jug of water down to help him out."

"That sounds much too simple and straightforward for Miss S."

"It is. When young Colveden got there he found the chap in something of a state. The bonnet of the van had fallen on his head, he'd burned his hands on the engine block or something, and tripped up and twisted his ankle."

The assistant commissioner dropped the putter onto the carpet, straightened up, and sighed with satisfaction. "That's more like it. Miss Seeton's work, undoubtedly."

"Ranger thought so when he heard about it, sir. When they discussed it, Colveden recalled her saying something about taking some vaseline with him as well as the water—for his hands, presumably—but he hadn't paid much attention at the time. So she might well have had a hand in that particular series of mishaps. Anyway, the radiator really had run dry, so Colveden filled it up and sent the man on his way. Not exactly rejoicing I imagine, but more or less fit to drive."

"So what, apart from the fact that something prompted Miss Seeton to set about him, was suspicious about this chap?"

"Had a most peculiar way of talking, Colveden told Ranger. Otherwise ordinary enough, in the sense that he looked like the sort of bloke who might well drive a clapped-out van. Possibly a market trader, middle-aged, ferrety-looking little chap, nondescript clothes. But he had this weird accent, it seems. As though he was trying to sound posh but didn't know how."

"Hm. Why would he want to do that, I wonder?"

"There's a lot of ifs and buts about this, sir, but Ranger theorizes that *if*—as Miss Seeton's sketches suggest—there's a connection between the Plummergen church job and the Thumper blackmailing affair, and *if* the gang involved saw Amelita Forby's piece in the *Negative* about Miss Seeton—"

"Hold your horses a minute. I thought we were all more or less agreed that we're looking for a man with a grievance acting alone."

"So we are, but if we're right, he's also done time, and might easily have made some friends in jail. Chief Inspector Brinton down in Ashford's responsible for the investigation of the church burglaries, and he's convinced they were organized by a pro."

"Not sure I follow you, but let it go for now. You inclined to go along with your chap Ranger's theory? Sounds a bit farfetched to me."

"He's not normally given to flights of fancy, sir. At all events, he's passed on the information such as it is to Mr. Brinton, and the Kent police will no doubt interview Nigel Colveden and get his firsthand description of the man."

"Why not get Miss S. to draw a picture of him?"

"Ranger's rather hoping she might do that spontaneously, sir. He'll keep in touch with her."

"Well, I suppose you know what you're about, but I must say it all sounds very vague and unsatisfactory to me. Sketches or no sketches, we're no nearer to identifying this blighter Miss Seeton claims to have seen at the Hurlingham Club."

"Oh, but we are."

"What? Have you been holding out on me, Delphick? I take a very poor view—"

"Wouldn't dream of it, sir. I only got confirmation myself shortly before I came to see you. I'm pretty sure the man we're after is one William Parsons. His name's on our list, I'm glad to report, so we'd have got round to him eventually—"

"Without Miss Seeton's help, you mean? Unworthy of you, Delphick. Give credit where credit's due, that's my motto. Including, needless to say, to you and your team."

Delphick inclined his head. "Sorry, sir. I deserved that. The man Parsons was formerly a branch manager for the Reliable Building Society. He came up before Mr. Justice Thumper on embezzlement charges, and Thumper sent him down for eight years. With maximum good conduct reduction, he was released in early December last year, shortly before Thumper thinks he started receiving the anonymous letters."

"Was he now. And do we know the present whereabouts of this Parsons?"

"We do. He's employed as an ambulance driver by Sussex County Council, based at a place called Cranhurst."

"Ambulance man, eh? Just as Miss Seeton said."

"Actually, she specified St. John's, but it's near enough to be highly significant, certainly."

"Going to pull him in for questioning, of course."

"With your permission, sir, I'd like to wait for a day or two before doing that. As I explained, we've only just got him into our sights, and I'd like to be in possession of more background when we do nab him. Talk to his probation officer, for example. He or she won't show us the file, of course, but might be willing to provide a verbal picture of the man. Some indication as to why he in particular among what one might call Thumper's victims—"

"One might, but one jolly well better hadn't. Her Majesty's judges enjoy high privileges and are inclined to be touchy about them. I didn't hear that remark, Delphick."

"And I didn't make it. It would, nevertheless, be useful

to find out if Parsons is known to have any particular reason to feel hostile to Sir Wilfred, or to harbor any grudge against his daughter."

"How's the girl holding up, by the way? Any problems in that department?"

"None whatever, I gather. Nigel Colveden implied to Ranger that there's quite a romance developing between them. And they set off in his car as usual this morning for her practice session, with a discreet Kent police escort laid on by Mr. Brinton."

"All right. What are you proposing to do exactly, then? Apart from pumping this man's probation officer?"

"Get hold of the transcript of his trial if it can be dug up. Send a man to the prison to have a word with any of the screws, beg pardon, sir, warders, who might remember Parsons. Above all, try to tie him directly to Hurlingham and to Plummergen on the relevant dates. If only negatively, by establishing that he *could* have been there. If it turns out that he was on duty on both occasions and can prove it, we'll be back to square one. Needless to say, I'm having an eye kept on him from now on, but as discreetly as possible so as to avoid putting him on the alert. If he is our man, with any luck he might lead us to his associates, and wander into our hands of his own free will."

"Very well. I'll go along with that so long as you can give me a hundred percent guarantee that no harm will come to the Thumper girl."

"She'll be watched like a hawk, sir."

"People don't watch hawks, Delphick. Other way round. Caught you out there. All right, off you go and do it your way, but keep me posted."

"Thank you. I will."

Sir Hubert let Delphick get as far as the door before speaking again. "I say, Delphick?"

"Sir?"

"These photocopies of Miss Seeton's sketches. Interesting, very. Where are the originals?"

"The originals? In a safe place, sir."

"Well, that's as far as we've got so far. What? Oh, thanks. I must admit it's a significant advance on last Saturday. Even my assistant commissioner here seems reasonably satisfied." Delphick sat back comfortably in his chair. Talking to Chris Brinton over the phone was a lot less demanding than being in the presence of Sir Hubert Everleigh.

"Quite. Oh, a day or two at most, obviously can't let it drag on. Needless to say, whatever we dig up I'll pass on to you personally. What I particularly wanted to talk to you about was this, though. Everleigh's given me the leeway I asked for, but reasonably enough insists that the protective cover on the girl must be watertight. Now when I dropped in on Sir George Colveden the other day he mentioned that the Rytham Hall lot are all invited to Glyndebourne tomorrow as Thumper's guests."

Brinton's response was immediate and eloquent, and Delphick waited patiently until he ran out of breath.

"I see you've already heard. Yes, of course it's tiresome for you, but if Colveden's already talked to your chief constable about it, that lets you out if something does go wrong, doesn't it. The problem is that from my point of view I'm afraid it isn't good enough for Sir George to insist that you call off your chaps for the evening. So what I propose is to have a quiet word with a contact of mine in the Sussex police and see if he can insert a couple of plainclothes men into the Glyndebourne grounds at least, and possibly the opera house itself, to keep an eye on the Thumper party. Be on the safe side, even though I can't imagine that anybody would be so daft as to try to get at Trish there."

"But I can't possibly get at the Thumper girl at a place like Glyndebourne," Parsons protested. "There'll be hundreds of people around."

"You can with me an' 'Arvey to 'elp. Listen, mate, I bin through a lot o' grief on your account, so you can leave it off comin' the smarmy Cuthbert with me. I'm tellin' you, that ol' cow's a bleedin' public menace, an' I got plans for 'er one o' these fine days. Meantime I'm 'andin' you this bird on a plate an' I'm not takin' no for an answer."

The two men were sitting in the pub at Cranhurst where they had met previously, and Parsons glanced again at Norman's bandaged hands. He had already noticed the slight limp and the way Norman gingerly touched the back of his neck from time to time.

"I appreciate the information, and what you're offering. Honestly. But I don't see how I can do a thing about it. To start with, there'll be regular Red Cross or St. John's volunteers on duty there."

"So you go in yer reggeler uniform, cloth-'ead. In yer amberlance. This opera place is in yer own manor, innit? Seven, eight miles away?"

"Well, yes, but—"

"Am I 'earin' the same geezer what pulled off that sweet little job at the tennis match? Pull yerself together, an' 'ear me out. Nah this is what we're gonna do, see . . ."

Reluctantly at first, but with gradually increasing interest, Parsons listened to Norman. Neither of them noticed the sallow young man with the lank, greasy hair who had slouched into the pub shortly after Parsons, bought himself a pint, and stationed himself at a pin-table machine not far away.

Even if they had, one glance at his ripped old leather jacket, unsavory-looking jeans, and dirty shoes would have been enough to keep them off guard. That, plus the fact that the young man was muttering obscenities to himself and furtively shoving at the machine to try to get it to behave differently, but not furtively enough to escape the eagle eye of the barman who shouted at him that if he felt like pushing he could push off.

In short, even to an experienced old hand like Norman, there was nothing whatever about Detective Constable Julian ''Sleaze'' Arbuthnott's appearance or manner to suggest that he might be a police officer, or that the packet of cigarettes protruding from the back pocket of his jeans contained a miniature tape recorder.

chapter 15

HAVING MADE several other telephone calls during the course of the morning, Mel Forby replaced the receiver this time with an air of finality and turned to Thrudd Banner, a triumphant smile on her face. "Pay up, you owe me a pound. Something to bear in mind for the future, lover boy. When I bet money on my chances of doing something, I don't reckon on losing it. Glyndebourne tickets are not to be had for love nor money, the man said. Forget it, Forby, he suggested, you'll just be wasting your time. Well, a pair of tickets will be waiting for us to pick up at the box office when we get there. Meet the *Negative*'s new music critic. We shall just have time to rush to London, get into our glad rags—you do *possess* a dinner jacket, I suppose—and make the train from Victoria to Lewes."

Banner examined the contents of his right-hand jacket pocket, extracted a crumpled pound note, folded it carefully, and inserted it into the front of her blouse. "Music critic forsooth! I'm beginning to wonder just what it is you have on that editor of yours, the way he jumps when you say jump. You know as much about opera as the average *Negative* reader does, which is that when some guy stabs another guy, they both sing."

"Not in this one they don't. It's Cavalli's *La Calisto*, and the stars are Ileana Cotrubas and Janet Baker. Far as I know neither one does any stabbing, and if you think those two dishy creatures're guys, then you haven't been paying attention these last few nights."

"Okay, you win. I still want to know why you came back from your walk this morning all fired up with the idea of going to Glyndebourne."

"If you'd come with me, you'd already know. I have my sources in Plummergen, mister, and a good journalist shouldn't reveal them. But now I've fixed the tickets I don't mind coming clean. I met Bob Ranger. He was out taking the air, too, and we got talking. Now that he knows we know about the Trish Thumper thing, he's loosened up. Admitted that he's going to Glyndebourne himself to keep an unobtrusive eye on Trish. Then it came out that he's taking Miss Seeton along, too."

"So what? A huge guy like Bob prowling around on his own would stick out a mile, so he needs a companion. Maybe Anne can't get away from the clinic. Miss S. will be perfect cover for him."

"Dear Thrudd, you're just too nice to smell a rat, aren't you? No. If Bob Ranger's been put on bodyguard duty, it's by Delphick. And Delphick must have his reasons for wanting him to take Miss S. along. Reasons he *didn't* have as recently as yesterday."

"How do you know?"

"Because I dropped in at Sweetbriars yesterday to see how Miss S. was feeling. She'd heard about the Rytham Hall crowd's plans for Glyndebourne when she had lunch there on Sunday, and said she hoped the weather would stay nice for them, particularly as Trish's parents are meeting them there. I didn't pay too much attention at the time, but now I recall that she sounded a little wistful. She definitely didn't expect to be going herself or she would have said so."

"Let me get this straight. Nigel's been driving Trish in his own car to and from Eastbourne for her training sessions, and the Kent police have been escorting them, right?"

"Sure. The escort's supposed to be invisible, but it's common knowledge. As is the fact that Nigel's goofy about Trish and seems to be getting somewhere with her."

"So presumably Brinton will have a car trailing the Colvedens to Glyndebourne this afternoon."

"Seems reasonable. With Bob and Miss S. aboard, perhaps."

"Okay. Now I can understand Delphick wanting Bob Ranger on parade just to provide routine protection for Trish inside the Glyndebourne grounds, especially if her dad's due to show up as well. But why on earth would he want Miss S. there, too?"

Mel deliberately made herself go cross-eyed, and aimed an imaginary pistol at him. "Because he thinks something's going to happen, dummy!"

"Amelita my flower, you're magnificent when you're angry. What, for example?"

"How in the world would I know what? But I'll bet you Delphick's setting something up."

"No bets. I've lost enough money to you today."

"Very wise. Anyhow, whatever it is, he won't have told Ranger in case he lets something slip to Miss Seeton. If I'm right, it's Miss S. that Delphick's counting on, and she always operates most spectacularly when she hasn't a clue what's happening."

"You know, I think that's about the craziest theory I've ever heard even you come up with. So you could just possibly be right. Okay, I'll indulge you."

"Do that thing, Banner. And bring your camera."

• • •

"I can of course imagine how busy Anne must be in these last few days before the wedding, but what a *great* pity she wasn't able to go with you today!"

It was the second time that Miss Seeton had made this point since being picked up by Ranger in the unmarked police car made available to him at Delphick's request by Chief Inspector Brinton. There being no conceivable way in which he could at short notice have got hold of a dinner jacket and trousers to fit him, and having been assured by Delphick that evening dress was optional at Glyndebourne nowadays, Bob was resplendent in the new dark suit he hadn't reckoned to wear until he took Anne to some smart restaurant during their honeymoon. Advised of this in advance, Miss Seeton had hastily consulted Lady Colveden by telephone and as a result put on her single string of pearls and best blue silk dress. The one Meg Colveden referred to as "that pretty cocktail dress you wore when you came for drinks on George's birthday."

"Not really. Anne's not much of a one for opera. Whereas you are, I know. I say, isn't that the Colvedens ahead?" In fact Ranger had fully expected to catch them up, having had a quiet word with Nigel who was to drive the big family Rover.

"I do believe it is. Yes, I can see Sir George and Lady Colveden in the back, so Patricia must be sitting beside Nigel in front. Oh dear, I hope so much that Sir George won't find it tedious, the opera, that is."

"I see what you mean. It's hardly likely to be his cup of tea, I suppose. On the other hand, it is his friend who's laid on the whole thing."

"Sir Wilfred Thumper, you mean. Such an unhappy man, don't you think?"

"I've never met him, but judging from that sketch you

drew and all I hear, he's certainly not exactly a barrel of laughs. Probably because nobody likes him. And whose fault is that? From all accounts he goes out of his way to make himself disagreeable."

"But not, it would appear, to Sir George. Don't you find that interesting, Mr. Rang—I mean, Bob?" Miss Seeton waved, having seen first Lady Colveden's head turn and then her husband's, and smiled in satisfaction when her gesture was acknowledged.

"Well, they go back a long way. Sir George probably thinks of him the way he was rather than the way he is."

"You're right. That *is* Ranger behind us, by crikey. Got up like a blessed undertaker. And Miss Seeton with him. Where on earth are they off to, d'you suppose?"

"Why, Glyndebourne, of course. Didn't I tell you, George? Miss Seeton rang me this morning to say Sergeant Ranger had got hold of a couple of tickets and invited her. He'd explained that he didn't have any evening dress with him and she asked me what I thought she ought to wear."

"Lucky beggar. To be able to wear an ordinary suit. While you made Nigel and me climb into these wretched penguin outfits."

"I think you look smashing, Sir George."

"Do you really, m'dear? Well, jolly nice of you to say so. Did you hear what Patricia just said, Nigel?"

Nigel glanced at the image reflected by the rearview mirror. "I heard, and stop stroking your moustache in that odious way, Dad. You look like some Edwardian masher," he added in a friendlier tone, much cheered when Trish surreptitiously squeezed his thigh.

"Patricia's quite right," Lady Colveden said. "And you look very nice too, dear. Men are always so impressive in dinner suits."

"All the same, Ma, it does make one feel an awful chump dressing up like this in broad daylight. And then going for a drive in the country. Oh well, at least if we get a puncture, Bob Ranger can change the wheel for us."

"It must be worse for the ones that go by train from London, I should think," Trish suggested, leaving her hand where it was.

"Perhaps, but on the other hand they all catch the same one so they've got plenty of company. Like when you see all the morning suits and gray toppers off to Ascot. You're very quiet, George."

"Quiet? Of course I'm quiet, haven't been able to get a word in edgeways. Besides, I'm thinkin'."

This was true. The proprietor of Rytham Hall was thinking that it was dashed cunning of that fellow Delphick to fix up his sergeant with a couple of tickets to the opera so that young Patricia there should not be put in any way at risk by his, George Colveden's, damn pigheadedness; and the thought that six feet seven inches of Bob Ranger was on hand was comforting. Getting the chief constable to tell Brinton to call off his flatfoots for the evening had seemed rather a dashing thing to do at the time. He had soon repented of it, but would have felt a complete ass to have gone cap in hand to Brinton and said so.

Nice for Miss Seeton to have a bit of an outing, too. Odd how one had become quite attached to the dotty old soul, with her extraordinary talent for getting herself into scrapes of one sort and another. Poor as a church mouse, of course, and barely knee-high to a grasshopper, but she must definitely have been officer material in her day. Amazing the way she'd brushed off that nasty business in the church, full of beans as usual over Sunday lunch.

Well, better keep an eye on her at Glyndebourne, make sure she didn't do any damage with that confounded umbrella of hers, and leave Ranger to watch out for any blighter sidling too close to young Thumper's girl.

William Parsons took one hand off the wheel and wiped his sweaty palm on his shirt, then repeated the process with the other. He was both excited and nervous, and barely in control of himself or the ambulance. It was one thing to have plotted and schemed for so long, a quite different matter to be on the point of turning a dream into reality.

Sending the letters had done little to assuage the burning need to hurt the bastard Thumper, the obsession he had nourished for so many years. Even the satisfaction of carrying off that brilliant exploit at the Hurlingham Club had not been as longlasting as he'd expected it to be, though it was wonderful to know that Thumper was running sufficiently scared to have put the girl into what the fool imagined to be a safe place and persuaded the police to provide protection. Now, so long as—

"Watch it, mate! Pull up, pull up, yer flippin' maniac! An' then come round the back 'ere. Wanna word with yer." The sliding communicating panel between the driving cab and the back of the ambulance had been left open so that Harvey and Norman could talk to him, but Parsons had been so immersed in his private thoughts that he had quite forgotten their presence. Now he glanced wildly round, saw the agitated, sharp-featured little face in the opening, realized that the ambulance was veering off the road, and righted it. Then he brought it to a halt, got out of the cab, and walked, sweating, to the back of the vehicle. One of the double doors was open, and Norman and Harvey were sitting side by side on the red blanket of the stretcher-bed glaring at him.

To put it more precisely, Norman was glaring at him,

while Harvey, his eyes closed, seemed to be whimpering quietly to himself. Norman, who was wearing a dark roll-necked sweater and jeans, spoke more quietly than before, in not much more than a hoarse whisper, but with a compelling intensity. ''Listen 'ere, mad-brain, an' listen good. 'Arvey an' me, we don't give a cuss if you wanna write yerself off, s'long as yer do it all on yer tod, right? But while me an' 'im are on board, be'ave yerself.''

Harvey shuddered delicately and opened his eyes. He looked very pale, and rather ethereal in his beautiful white dinner jacket, worn with a frilled shirt and a pink bow tie and cummerbund that delicately emphasized the blush-tone of his hair. ''My dear William,'' he began in a sad, long-suffering tone. ''I cannot now remember how I allowed myself to be persuaded to join you in this insane venture, and my stomach is much too upset for me to try. So please, dear boy, bear in mind that if you value my good-will and future cooperation, you must drive us sedately from here, at no time exceeding a speed of thirty miles per hour, until we are safely inside the purlieus of Glyndebourne.''

''Or else we'll knock yer flippin' block off,'' Norman added succinctly. ''Got that?''

''I'm sorry,'' Parsons said humbly enough, though Norman didn't like the bloodshot look of his eyes, or the way his hands were twitching.

''All right, then. Understandable yer a bit uptight, but get a grip, mate. Got yer patter worked out if anybody challenges yer?''

''I have. And please don't refer to this as an insane venture, Harvey. I don't care for that word.'' Parsons closed the rear door quietly and the two passengers stared at each other, listening to the crunch of his footsteps outside.

"Norman, I have a sinking feeling that our friend really is off his trolley."

"Too bleedin' right 'e is. Yer know, I'm beginnin' to wonder if we done the right thing."

chapter
~16~

As a connoisseur not only of English silver but of the finer things in life in general, Harvey had been to Glyndebourne before. He was therefore familiar with the unconventional timing of the performances given there, the very early start allowing for the seventy-five minute dinner interval during which those opera lovers who didn't patronize the restaurant picnicked elegantly in the grounds. So Harvey it was who had telephoned to inquire the precise timings for *La Calisto* that evening, and ordained that they should arrive a few minutes before the beginning of that interval, at a time when very few people would be wandering about outside.

It was a wise decision. There was nobody in sight when William Parsons, sweating and trembling with the effort to behave normally, piloted the ambulance slowly and with exaggerated care through the main entrance and into the restricted parking area near the splendid country house and its associated auditorium. Positioning the vehicle in such a way that the rear doors were concealed from general view, he climbed down from the driving seat, walked round to the back after checking that the coast was still clear, and opened the door to allow Harvey to slip out. Harvey's forehead was damp with perspiration, too, and he looked very pale, but he took a deep breath, straightened his dinner jacket and cummerbund over his enviably flat stomach, and then sauntered with a creditable show of nonchalance into the garden.

No more than two or three minutes later the doors of the auditorium were opened, the audience began to stream out, and Harvey was soon drifting as unobtrusively as his *avant garde* hairstyle permitted among the dozens of people pottering about, sniffing the air, admiring the herbaceous borders and chatting animatedly about the stage design, costumes, and performance. As always on these occasions, there were those who considered that their opinions ought to be made known to others in addition to their immediate companions, and whose voices were therefore pitched so as to be overheard.

Sir George Colveden was not one of these exhibitionists. His remarks were aimed solely at Sir Wilfred Thumper, and he fondly imagined himself to be delivering them in a discreet undertone. In this he was mistaken. Like most other members of the upper classes he had been brought up to speak out clearly and confidently; while the habit of command and long years of exercise on military parade grounds had so strengthened his vocal chords that he was invariably audible at a great distance.

"Quite frankly, can't imagine what you see in this sort of stuff, Thumper," he trumpeted. "Decent of you to stand us the tickets, of course, but wasted on me I'm afraid, old boy. Ah well, never mind, we've got Meg's picnic hamper to look forward to. Nice to see the memsahibs togged up in their best. Handsome gel, your Patricia. You're no oil painting, so she must get it from her mother's side, eh?"

Having emerged from a different exit, Miss Seeton and Bob Ranger were still at least thirty feet away as Sir George was holding forth, but still his voice rose effortlessly above the considerable hubbub of conversation all around. "Oh dear, Sir George isn't enjoying himself," said Miss Seeton.

"He sounds in pretty good form to me, the way he's teasing the judge," Bob assured her. "Not something that happens to him all that often, I should say."

"Well, I'm sure Sir Wilfred knows him well enough not to be offended." She rummaged in her capacious bag and produced a neatly wrapped package. "Now, these sandwiches that Martha has been so kind as to make for us. We might perhaps take them to the lakeside, do you think? Oh dear, I've just thought. How very remiss of me not to have provided a bottle of wine to accompany them. That is, I believe it's considered the thing to do, and you have been so generous—oh *dear*!"

"Not a bit of it, Miss S. I'm driving, remember, and in any case—" Bob just managed to stop himself from adding the ritual phrase about not drinking while on duty.

"Hark at old Colveden," Thrudd Banner said to Mel Forby. They were standing on the other side of the garden entirely, but there was scarcely a breath of wind and they, too, were well within earshot. "Marvelous old buffer, as honest as the day is long. I wonder how many other people in these grounds feel that way about opera, too, but wouldn't dream of admitting it."

Mel assumed a haughty expression and looked down her nose at him. "Kindly remember you're here as the guest of a distinguished music critic. Hey, and don't hog all that chocolate, by the way. It's going to have to last a long time. I enjoyed the first act a lot, if you want to know."

"So did I, to tell you the truth. Especially Janet Baker. Had to keep reminding myself why we're here." He touched her hand briefly. "Must be getting sentimental. Well, I guess we'd better keep Trish Thumper and her doting pa in sight. How many other people have her under surveillance, d'you reckon?"

"Wow, let me think. Bob Ranger for one. Miss Seeton, although nobody's actually told her that's what she's here for."

"No need to."

"Right. Plus us two. And it wouldn't surprise me in the least if it turns out that Delphick's arranged for some muscle to be lurking in the undergrowth in case of need. Then we mustn't forget Mister X, the guy who's out to get Trish or her old man or both."

A good many other people registered Sir George Colveden's remarks. Some smiled in a superior fashion, a few giggled, and others affected to ignore them. Harvey paid close attention, pleased to be confirmed in his provisional identification of the two elderly gentlemen, two middle-aged ladies, one young man, and one young woman in evening dress whom he had spotted coming out of the auditorium together. The young couple were dressed very differently from the way Norman had described them after seeing them passing Plummergen church in the little red MG sports car, but having studied a photograph of Trish Thumper taken from an *Illustrated London News* feature entitled "Britain's Wimbledon Hopefuls Face Strong Competition," Harvey hadn't been in much doubt. Now, hearing Sir George address his companion as Thumper and refer to the girl as Patricia made it definite. So now all he had to do was—oh, good grief, it didn't bear thinking about, especially as it now seemed they were mixed up with a lunatic.

Nigel Colveden, having been sent to the car to fetch the picnic hamper, arrived back at the lakeside to find that the senior Thumpers had been on an errand of their own, and returned with four small collapsible canvas-seated stools and two shooting-sticks. Lady Colveden began to unpack the hamper and lay out plates and cutlery on a cloth spread on the grass with Trish's help, while Sir Wilfred fussily arranged the stools and installed his silent wife on one of them. It was impossible to tell from Lady Thumper's expression what, if anything, she was thinking, but she seemed quite malleable and stayed quietly wherever she was put. Sir George had fixed one of the shooting-sticks into the turf, opened up the handles to form a seat, and was perched on it, surveying the scene with apparent satisfaction.

"Excellent. Here's the supplies officer arrived with the rations at last. Well done, Nigel. As a reward, you get to crouch on one of those little footstool gadgets, my boy. As you can see, I've bagged Thumper's spare shootin' stick for meself. Good idea of his to bring 'em along. And I say, some of these opera fanatics are a lot more sensible than they look, you know. See those little tent peg things stuck in the ground here and there by the edge of the lake, with strings tied to them? Bottles! Coolin' in the water! Been watchin' chaps fishin' 'em out. And what's more—"

"I have almost reconciled your father to the prospect of more opera to come, Coleveden, by informing him that I too placed a number of bottles in the lake immediately on arrival here." Sir Wilfred didn't exactly smile, but his habitually acid expression softened as he looked up at his former schoolmate.

"Well, I'm hanged if I can see anybody who looks particularly suspicious, can you?"

Banner shook his head. "Nope. A few weirdos, but not as many of those as you get even at Covent Garden, and that's a snobby place, too."

"That's because even the cheapest tickets here cost too much, and then you have train fare on top of that even if you don't dress up. The guy with the pink hair pussyfooting about's sort of cute, Thrudd. Why don't you get a shot of him, we might make the *Negative* buy it off you for large sums—no, wait, this'll be even better. Look, Miss Seeton's going over to have a word with the Colvedens and you'll be able to get the weirdo and Miss S. together in a great contrast . . ."

Having gritted his teeth and taken several deep breaths, Harvey finally summoned up the courage to go through with what he was now convinced was a truly crackpot scheme, and headed toward the party at the lakeside. It seemed a good moment, since the skinny old man—Thumper, he now knew, was bent forward facing the water, pulling gently on a piece of string with one hand and reaching with the other for the neck of the attached wine bottle which had just broken the surface. While the others, with the exception of the beefy-looking girl, had turned round to face the old biddy who was approaching them, beaming and obviously an acquaintance.

Patricia was giving her full attention to a leg of chicken, and barely glanced up when Harvey leaned over her, coughed deferentially, and spoke. "It *is* Trish Thumper, isn't it? I'm desperately sorry to intrude, Miss Thumper, but could you possibly come up to the house for a moment? You're wanted urgently on the phone. Something about Wimbledon, I believe."

Later there were to be conflicting explanations of what happened next. Sir George stoutly averred to his wife in the privacy of their bedroom that he wasn't taken in for a moment by the pink-haired apparition in the white dinner jacket, and "went a bit berserk, actually, like those Malayan johnnies used to. Made a lunge for the feller."

Miss Seeton, on the other hand, reflecting on the events in question in the company of Chief Superintendent Delphick, said that it was all most unfortunate, that she had intended simply to tuck her umbrella under her left arm in order to shake hands. With Lady Thumper, that is, who seemed rather out of things. And accidentally hooked it round Sir George's shooting stick. The handle, of course. Of the umbrella. One had often admired the way gentlemen—and ladies too, needless to say—seemed to be able to balance on those funny little seats. But inevitably it was all too easy for a person to be dislodged, as Mr. Delphick would no doubt agree.

Bob Ranger said that from his viewpoint some yards away it had struck him as a brilliantly conceived and executed maneuver on Miss S.'s part, and that what he would always remember most vividly was the sight of Lady Thumper of all people helpless with laughter.

Whatever the true explanation, the basic facts were not in doubt. These were that Sir George toppled heavily off his perch and bumped violently into Harvey, who in turn cannoned into Sir Wilfred, who in falling into the lake grabbed desperately at Harvey, taking him with him. That it was Harvey who first realized that the water was only chest-deep, managed to stand upright, and then drag Thumper to his feet, too. And that there they stood for a few seconds, Thumper clinging to the young man while Thrudd Banner took photograph after photograph with Mel Forby urging him on with cries of adoration.

It was Nigel Colveden who noticed in the midst of all the excitement that Trish was no longer among those present, looked around wildly, and then spotted her back a moment before it disappeared from view. Since everybody seemed to be talking at once he seized Sir Wilfred Thumper's now unoccupied shooting-stick and set off in pursuit of his beloved.

Trish was nowhere to be seen, but Nigel had overheard what the man had said to her and made for the house, pausing in an agony of indecision on realizing that it seemed to have a number of entrances, into any one of which Trish might have gone to speak to her anonymous, possibly fictitious telephone caller. It was as well that he did hesitate, for otherwise he might not have noticed anything odd about the ambulance parked nearby; but he did. It was rocking, lurching up and down on its springs.

Had he not been in an agitated state, this phenomenon might have amused Nigel. Having grappled from time to time with a young woman in the cramped confines of his little car, he had often thought longingly of the advantages of being able to spread oneself, as it were, in such situations. The thought that some lucky, amorous pair might be making use of a vehicle equipped with blacked out windows and what amounted to a proper bed would in different circumstances have excited Nigel's envious interest.

The thing was, though, that he was worried, and the lurching was accompanied by a series of thumps and muffled oaths that suggested a fight rather than even the most exuberant bout of lovemaking. So Nigel approached the back of the ambulance, the driver's door of which was open, and peeped through the gap between the back doors, which were ajar.

He was just in time to see Trish, majestic in her wrath, poised to hurl a small but presumably weighty cylinder of oxygen at a little man with sly, pinched-looking features. A man he had seen before, by the roadside near the gates of Rytham Hall, and even spoken to, after a fashion. Nigel watched him put up his arms to protect his head, but Trish's improvised missile nevertheless found its mark and her victim made an odd little noise midway between a squeak and a yelp and collapsed over the body of a second man, already lying in a heap on the floor.

Nigel wrenched both doors open and gazed at the spectacularly heaving bosom of the panting, wild-eyed woman within. "Gosh, Trish, are you all right?" he inquired. As a remark, it was hardly the stuff of romance, but it seemed to hit the spot. Trish blinked at him, at first in a sort of daze, but then shyly, after she had glanced down at the gaping front of her dress and drawn it together, but not as quickly as all that.

"You came after me, Nigel!" she then murmured as Bob Ranger pounded up to join them, accompanied by Detective Constable "Sleaze" Arbuthnott and a rather more stalwart-looking colleague of his. "You *are* sweet, aren't you?"

chapter

–17–

"SINGING LIKE canaries," Brinton said. "At least, my pair of beauties have been, ever since the Sussex boys handed them over. Honor among thieves? Tell that to the marines. Pretty Boy blames it all on his mate. Led astray, he was. Innocent young lad straight out of college, started at the bottom in one of those posh auction houses. Sotheby's? Doing well, learning the trade, swotted up on hallmarks and so forth, makes himself quite the little expert on silver. So they put him on the 'in off the street' counter. You know, Oracle. Little old ladies popping in with their shopping bags, Great Aunt Fanny's favorite teapot wrapped up in newspaper, wonder if it might be worth a quid or two."

"You're not trying to tell me this Norman Proctor joined the queue one day to price his family heirlooms, are you?"

"Not on your nelly. No, Pretty Boy has this little personal problem, see? Well, hardly a problem, just something he can't very well discuss with his Mum, who's wondering why he never seems to bring any nice girls home for tea. It's because he's much happier spending his evenings at this quiet little club he belongs to, where there's a lot more like him and he's much in demand."

Delphick enjoyed a good story as much as the next man,

but he had rather a lot to do and was finding Brinton's ponderous humor somewhat wearisome. "So Proctor's gay too, is he? I'm surprised to hear that."

"No, no, you've got the wrong end of the stick there."

"Point out the right end then, Chris. Sorry to rush you, but I've got rather a lot on my plate at the moment."

"Oh, all right then, if you must rain on my parade. As we both very well know, it wasn't so long ago that blokes could go to jail for doing what comes naturally to lads like our Harvey. When he got into the gay scene it was illegal, and quite a bit of cash was skimmed off by characters who were bent in more ways than one. Harvey met crooks, and when they found out about his professional talents he got persuaded into doing a bit of freelance appraising work on the side. Word got around, Proctor needed an expert partner, got in touch, and Bob's your uncle. He's told us all about the church jobs and where the stuff's stashed away, but claims he never wanted to go in for any rough stuff or kidnapping. That was all Proctor's idea, according to him."

"*Proctor's*?"

"Yeah. Said that Parsons is a nutter, obsessed with some harebrained scheme to snatch the Thumper bird."

"Yes, yes, we all know that."

"No need to bite my head off, Oracle. Hear me out, I'm telling you Harvey's side of it. That he and Proctor had intended to drop Parsons like a hot brick after the church jobs, until they found out that it was Miss Seeton they'd tangled with, and got nervous. Then Proctor found out that the whole boiling of 'em were going to be at Glyndebourne, practically just down the road from where Parsons works. So cooked up the idea that the pair of them would pretend to go along with Parsons and help him snatch the girl, but then shop him. Do a deal, see? Return Thumper's kid and hand Parsons to us on a plate, provided we agree to forget about the burglaries."

"That's a preposterous yarn if I ever heard one."

"I've heard weirder ones in my time. Anyway, Pretty Boy seems to believe it. And seems to reckon that if he grasses on his mate, we might go easy on him as a first offender."

"Does he indeed? I'm sure you couldn't possibly have encouraged him in that assumption, could you, Chris? What does Proctor have to say?"

"His version's a lot different from Harvey's, needless to say. He accepts that with a form sheet like his he's bound to cop another dose of porridge, but he doesn't fancy being done for bodily harm, assault, and attempted kidnapping any more than Harvey does. So his line is he's just a small-time burglar who happened to share a cell with this educated, Svengali type Parsons and got drawn into his wicked schemes. That it was Parsons who attacked Miss S., Parsons who masterminded the plan to nab Trish Thumper, and so on and so forth. And that N. Proctor was a helpless pawn in his hands, and is the poor innocent victim of grievous bodily harm committed against his person by the aforementioned T. Thumper. He's certainly got a whopper of a lump on the side of his napper to prove it."

"Well, all I can say is the best of British luck to you, Chris. All very interesting, but it just makes everything look all the more complicated from where I sit."

"Can't see why. Aren't you going to tell me how you're doing with your baby?"

"To tell you the truth, not very well at all. Parsons is admitting nothing. In fact he's saying nothing. He'll be remanded for medical examination, of course. Not physical, Trish Thumper did him no great harm when she clobbered him. But his mental state's bound to be a factor when he comes up for full trial. It's entirely possible he'll be judged unfit to plead."

"Proctor claims he's an evil genius, Harvey reckons he's barmy, like I said. What's your verdict?"

"Wouldn't like to say at this stage. There are more immediate problems to cope with, anyway."

"Oh?"

"Yes indeed. As things stand, his employers, namely the Sussex County Ambulance Service, could bring charges against him for unauthorized use of their vehicle, and damaging or permitting others to damage its interior. And I suppose you could rope him in as an accessory to the church burglary jobs. But that's all."

"Am I hearing you right, Oracle? What about the assault on Miss S.? The attempted kidnapping of the girl? The threatening letters to her old man?"

"No charges, it seems."

"No *charges*? You're having me on."

"Nope."

"But Miss S.'s already identified Parsons as the bloke that jumped her in the church! Be your age, that was what broke the case for us!"

"I know, but she doesn't want us to prosecute him. She had a long talk with Ranger this morning. Likewise Trish Thumper. And although I haven't the slightest idea yet what grounds she had for saying so, Trish Thumper told Ranger quite definitely that her father wouldn't be taking the matter any further either."

"What the blazes has been going on?"

"I don't know, but I mean to find out. I'm going down to Plummergen myself later today. All Ranger could tell me was that after the fiasco by the lake—I tell you Chris, I'm furious with myself for not being there to see it—and the brawl in the ambulance, the whole Plummergen gang reasonably enough abandoned the opera and headed for home. Accompanied by a very subdued Wilfred Thumper, wearing the picnic tablecloth like a sarong and the jacket of Bob Ranger's new suit, about which Ranger's very fed up. That journalist chap, Banner, drove the judge, Lady Thumper, and Mel Forby in the Thumper car. Ranger took Miss Seeton, who insisted that he should drop her off at Rytham Hall with the others."

"Oh boy, must have been a right old circus when they all arrived. So they put old Thumper into a hot bath, tucked him up in bed afterwards, and then Miss S. and Trish got their heads together and for some mysterious reasons of their own decided to muck everything up for us. That what you think happened?"

"It's all I can think, at the moment. Keep all this under your hat, Chris. I'll try to keep you in the picture, but until I know what it is myself I don't want you or anybody else going off the deep end."

"Hurry up, the suspense has been killing me!" The moment Thrudd entered the door Mel jumped up from the tiny dressing table in her room at the George and Dragon, rushed into his arms, and contrived simultaneously to hug him and to deprive him of the large buff envelope he had been carrying. She nodded her head toward her portable typewriter precariously balanced on the dressing table.

"I've been trying to draft a story, but I couldn't concentrate. You've been a heck of a long time, lover." She drew out the contents of the envelope and studied them for a few moments. Then, unable to maintain her poker face any longer, she treated him to a smile of pure delight. "Thrudd, you're a genius. You're forgiven for having that smug smile on your face when you walked in here."

"Not bad, are they? I had quite a job persuading the guy

that runs the photographic studio in Brettenden to do the job at all, let alone to rush it. Said he specialized in weddings, children, and pets and had an urgent date with a cocker spaniel. But after I spoke to him about the power of the press he agreed to develop the film and run off the contacts and a few enlargements, by special arrangement with money."

"Who's a clever boy, then? Wowee!" Having spread out the enlargements on the bed, Mel scrutinized with more care the sheet of contact prints she held in her hand.

"I just had him blow up the obvious ones, but there are a few others that might be of interest."

Mel put down the contacts and stood beside the bed head down, poring over the enlargements. "My only regret is that newspapers can't run pics in color yet. It'll come, they do say. But I can't forget the way that guy's hair matched his bow tie. Thumper may be a dried-up old prune, but he sure has good taste in boyfriends. That shot's the prizewinner, if you want my opinion."

"Speaking as a music critic, you mean, or as a hotshot feature writer?" Thrudd closed in on Mel from behind, put his arms round her and nuzzled at her neck. Then he peered over her shoulder at the photograph she had indicated.

It was beautifully sharp, and depicted a sodden Harvey standing chest-deep in the waters of the lake at Glyndebourne, with an equally drenched Sir Wilfred Thumper apparently embracing him. The expression on the judge's clearly recognizable face must in fact have been one of shock and distress, but what Thrudd's lens had captured looked uncommonly like drunken affection.

"Passing lightly over that ungallant wisecrack, all we have to do now is figure out how best to use it. And also, incidentally, what the dickens your friend and mine Miss

Emily D. Seeton is up to. Did I give you permission to remove your arms, Mr. Banner?''

He put them back round her and squeezed. ''Oh Mel, you're so stern. You will be gentle with me, won't you?'' Then in his normal voice, ''*Is* Miss S. up to something?''

''You bet she is. I dropped in to see her this morning. She was as bright-eyed and bushy-tailed as ever.''

''Why shouldn't she be? She didn't get dunked in the lake. Just pushed everybody else in.''

''That wasn't the way she explained it, but never mind. She made me a cup of coffee, and we chatted. Agreed that it's great that the heat is well and truly off Trish Thumper, but Miss S. admitted that she was disappointed to have missed the rest of *La Calisto*. Then she looked at me kind of sideways in that perky way she does sometimes and said she and Trish had both been in touch with Bob Ranger first thing and told him they didn't intend to press charges against the man she calls Tintoretto. The ambulance driver.''

''They *what*?''

''You heard me. At least, not before they know all about him. Miss S. is convinced he has a secret sorrow, and she seems to have persuaded Trish to agree with her.''

''Darn right he has a secret sorrow, and I can guess what it is. He's sorry he ever got mixed up in this crazy affair, and he's even sorrier that he's going to spend years in jail because of it.''

''That remains to be seen. Delphick's coming down to Plummergen later today, presumably to reason with them.''

''But Mel, this is the character who's been making the lives of the entire Thumper family a misery. Even if Trish is misguided enough to try to let him get away with it, you can bet your boots old Sir Sourpuss won't.''

''We shall see. Anyway, it's just after twelve. Shall we go down and get some lunch, or what?''

"If the alternative is what I think it is, I'd prefer what."

"But Miss Seeton, justice really must take its course, you know."

"Oh, but I'm sure it will. Now that you have so kindly explained the background. To this unfortunate man's predicament, I mean. It was something about the eyes, you know. Trish—such a dear child—understood immediately when I explained it to her."

"I grant you that it was a sad case, but there was cast-iron evidence that Parsons did make off with that money."

"So he did, but most ineptly, according to what you have told me. And come now, Mr. Delphick, it was recovered within an hour or two. Not so much as a pennyworth of interest was lost to the building society. The Reliable, I believe. Such an attractive, straightforward name. You know, I often wonder how many members of the one called the Woolwich Equitable use *that* adjective on a day-to-day basis. If Mr. Parsons so far forgot himself as to behave in an *unreliable* way, why, that was no doubt because he was distracted. A good many years ago I myself was shocked to discover that I had inadvertently removed a book from a public library without having it stamped. And I was only thinking about quill pens at the time, not desperately worried about a beloved daughter."

"Hard cases make bad law, Miss Seeton."

"What a very silly maxim that is. It was by Pearl Buck, I remember, and turned out not to be at all to my taste. The book, that is, so I took it back. Well, a principle like that might appeal to Sir Wilfred Thumper, but I have no time for it."

"It's not like you to be so vehement, Miss Seeton."

"Vehement. A fairly uncommon word. Now *you'd* have

no trouble with one like 'equitable', Mr. Delphick. I do admire it. Your vocabulary, I mean. But I admit that I do. Feel strongly. Such a very distressing story. That poor, wretched man!''

''That man *attacked* you. And he planned at the very least to hold Trish Thumper captive. Quite possibly to harm her.''

Miss Seeton shook her head decisively.

''Not Tintoretto, Mr. Delphick. The beard is very full and quite conceals the chin, but I've already mentioned the eyes. I doubt it very much. That he would in fact have harmed Trish even if she had not demonstrated to him so conclusively that she is well able to take care of herself.'' She sighed gently. ''As for me, I still feel embarrassed. That I hurt him, while he did no more than frighten me a little. By hitting him with my torch, I mean. It was the other man who tied me up. The one with the van. With the absurd assumed accent. He was afraid, you see. That I should remember his voice.''

Delphick smiled. ''Yes. And I gather that in your own way you gave him cause to regret that second encounter, too. So am I now really to understand that you're disposed to forget the whole thing?''

''Oh dear, no! Poor Mr. Parsons lost his daughter in frightful circumstances. The child he loved so dearly that he courted professional and personal ruin. In an attempt to help her. And then the poor man was subjected to unnecessary public humiliation by an odious bully. Something must be done.''

''Strong words, Miss Seeton,'' Delphick said, fascinated by this unfamiliar, crusading side to her.

''Well, you see, so much unhappiness flowed from it. The trial. I quite see that Sir Wilfred Thumper isn't accountable. For the death of that poor child, I mean. But blameworthy, certainly. It is understandable, isn't it, Mr. Delphick? That Mr. Parsons, during years of frightful mental anguish, should have made him the focus of his bitter desire for revenge?''

''Perhaps it is understandable, but I don't quite see why Trish Thumper should be expected to display as much magnanimity as you. More or less on his own written admission, Parsons administered some noxious substance to her at the Hurlingham Club, which made her ill and resulted in her losing an important match.''

''Really, Mr. Delphick! She tells me that it was almost certainly nothing more than a strong laxative. Martha Bloomer swears by Eno's Fruit Salts herself, and certainly wouldn't call it noxious. She'd prefer California Syrup of Figs, but they don't seem to sell it these days, she says. And it was an exhibition match. Not in the least important.''

Delphick shook his head slowly and sighed. ''Well, I can see it's not much use arguing with you,'' he said. Then he stood up and prepared to leave. ''Thank you for the tea and cake, Miss Seeton. I must be off to Rytham Hall now. To see Sir Wilfred.''

''Really? I understand that apart from having caught a severe cold, he is none the worse for his experience. Rather the reverse, in fact.''

''That's a rather mysterious remark, Miss Seeton. Anyway, let me remind you that Parsons has subjected him to severe mental and emotional stress over a period of months. In spite of what his daughter said to Sergeant Ranger, I somehow doubt if Thumper Senior will be inclined to forgive and forget.''

Miss Seeton's previously serious expression had been replaced by something like a twinkle. ''Don't be too sure, Mr. Delphick,'' she said sweetly.

chapter

–18–

It's not easy on the face of it to understand why it can make perfectly good sense to describe a rapping on a door as hesitant. Audible or inaudible, yes, but surely to go beyond that is fanciful? Not a bit of it. A moment's thought suffices to make the fair-minded person accept that, just as the occupant of a room would be fully justified in interpreting a succession of thunderous blows as menacing, or a rapid tattoo as peremptory or impatient, so the occupant of the library at Rytham Hall, namely Sir George Colveden, was quite right to infer that the taps he heard were tapped by a hesitant, not to say timid, tapper.

"Come in!" he called, and sat back to watch the doorknob turn and the door open, as if by no human agency. Then, in the gradually widening gap, a pale face appeared, half obscured by a wad of paper tissues being held beneath a nose in contrasting red.

"You, ah, wodted to see me, I understad, Colbeded."

"Ah, there you are, Thumper. Yes, as a matter of fact I did. Well, don't just stand there, come in, come in. That's better. Take a pew, old boy." Never one to shirk a disagreeable duty, Sir George had, following the telephone call from Miss Seeton, mentally prepared himself for the forthcoming interview. He nevertheless found his resolve weakening when he contemplated the shambling, sniffing figure of Sir Wilfred Thumper.

"Good God! Just realized I haven't set eyes on you since last night. You look perfectly frightful, man!"

"Bery sorry, Colbeded. But your wife gabe me this to wear."

"No, no, I don't mean that old dressing gown of mine. Even though I thought she'd given it to the Salvation Army or Oxfam or somebody like that years ago. You're welcome to it. Take it away with you if you like. No, I mean that streaming cold in the head. You ought to be in bed. Get the doctor to have a look at you, what?"

"Was in bed, Colbeded. But Labidia tode me to get up ad pull byself together." Sir Wilfred abandoned himself to a paroxysm of sneezing while Sir George gaped at him in disbelief.

"*Lavinia* did? That doesn't sound at all like her. And besides, since when did you pay any attention to Lavinia?" He paused in some confusion, and cleared his throat. "As you were, Thumper. Remark out of order, none of my business. Sorry about that. Anyway, you've got a corker of a cold there. Here, you'd better have a whiskey."

Sir George decided to have a bracer himself, too, and the business of going over to the side table and pouring them took long enough to enable him to think about and decide to revise the tactics he had planned to employ. Clearly a subtler approach was called for. The invalid accepted the drink with an air of humble gratitude.

"Bery good ob you."

"Think nothing of it. I say, Thumper, d'you remember that blighter Remington at all?"

"Rebigtod? Yes. Prefect. School House. Dot likely to forget."

"Ah, precisely! I should jolly well say not. Thoroughly bad lot, used to torment the junior boys. Accuse them of breaking all sorts of rules they never even knew existed. Because they didn't, of course. Used to stage mock trials, along with some of his cronies, and invent humiliating punishments just for their own amusement, that sort of thing."

"He did. Beastly sadist, you called hib. The tibe you rescued be, Colbeded."

Sir George blinked as his memory projected a vivid picture in his mind, of a half-empty storeroom at school, getting on for fifty years in the past. Of a group of sneering seniors centered round the unspeakable Remington, and of a skinny little boy standing before them with his short trousers down round his ankles, tears streaming down his face, and his quavering, piping voice breaking down repeatedly in his attempts to sing the comic song ordered by his tormentors. And of himself at sixteen or seventeen bursting into the room, taking in the scene, and roaring incoherently as he launched himself with arms flailing at Remington in defense of young Thumper, his fag.

"Gabe hib a bloody doze, you did. Ad two ob the others."

"So you do remember. Must admit I'm a bit surprised, in view of what I've learned today. I don't mind telling you that I'd been intending to read you the riot act this afternoon. And rather regretting that I'm no longer in a position to give you six of the best." Red-eyed and red-nosed, the former fag said nothing, but looked ever more woeful as Sir George pressed on. "I've been proud of you, young Thumper. Watched your career with interest and, yes, dammit, respect. No small thing to become one of Her Majesty's judges, after all. Knew you were said to be a tough nut, told myself a judge has to be firm. Didn't much admire the way I saw you treat Lavinia sometimes, but it doesn't do to speculate about other people's marriages, eh? Anyway, I never thought I'd have to face the fact that a former fag of mine turned out to be a bully. You've let me down, old boy."

"If you say so, Colbeded. I'b sorry, Colbeded."

"So I should hope. Well, it's never too late to mend. My understanding is that this fellow who wrote you those letters had every reason to give you a hard time. Agreed?"

"Perhaps, Colbeded, but—"

"No perhapses or buts about it. Did you know that both Miss Seeton and Patricia have decided not to press charges against him?"

"Yes, Colbeded. Patricia tode be."

"Good. Now, I gather Chief Superintendent Delphick's coming over here to see you shortly. What are you proposing to say to him?"

For the first time the light of defiance came into Sir Wilfred's inflamed eyes. "Justice bust be dud!" he insisted.

Mel Forby put the telephone down and turned to Thrudd. "I can't believe it," she said. "I don't recall Miss Seeton ever ringing me up before."

"She's all right, is she? Not sick or anything?"

"I don't think so. Just upset. Delphick just left her, his second visit today. To say that he'd talked to old Thumper, who says that no matter what she and Trish have decided, he wants the book thrown at this guy Parsons. For sending him a series of threatening letters."

"I'll be darned. He doesn't give up easy, does he?"

"Nope. Apparently Sir George, Trish, and even Lady Thumper have all had a go at him, but he's adamant."

"Lady Thumper? But hasn't he treated her like a doormat for years?"

"So they say, but apparently the sight of him taking a

header into the lake had an electrifying effect on her. Having been terrified of him for most of their married life, she suddenly realized that he's not a dignified, awe-inspiring figure at all. In fact, he's nothing but a pompous, ridiculous old poop who's been sponging off her money for far too long."

"Well, that's a useful blow for freedom, for a start. But if Miss Seeton says he's down but not out, I guess Parsons will have to face the music after all."

"Not necessarily," Mel said thoughtfully. Then she put up a hand and stroked his cheek with infinite tenderness. "Thrudd, darling?"

"State your business, Forby."

"I was just wondering . . ."

"You were just wondering how badly I want to sell that photograph of Thumper and his boyfriend to a French scandal mag. Right?"

"What a suggestion! Besides, he probably isn't his boyfriend."

"Who's to know? Anyhow, we can't allow Miss S. to get upset, especially not by a creep like Thumper. Shall I tell you what I think we ought to do? I think we ought to stroll up to Rytham Hall, ask to have a word with Sir Wilfred, and show him that pic."

"Mister *Banner!*" Mel looked properly shocked. "I'm surprised at you. Are you proposing to blackmail that poor old gentleman?"

"Sort of."

"Good. I was afraid you'd never get round to it."

"I can hear footsteps. And voices. Turn the light off, quickly, Norah."

"Well, that is the main street of the village out there, after all," Mrs. Blaine pointed out, but nevertheless did as she was bidden, and plunged the sitting room into darkness. Miss Nuttel then drew the curtain aside by an inch or two and peered out.

"Shh!"

"I *am* shishing, Eric."

"*. . . oh boy, am I glad you're here!*"

"*Couldn't have done without me, sweetheart, could you? I wonder if Bob Ranger's in on all this?*"

"*The latest twist, you mean? I doubt . . .*" The voices faded into the distance.

"There! What did I tell you?"

"You didn't tell me anything. Can I put the light back on now?"

"Very well, I suppose so."

Blinking, Mrs. Blaine observed the satisfied smile on her friend's face. "Well, who was it, then?"

"The Forby creature. With her paramour, Banner."

"I say, do you really think he's her paramour?" Mrs. Blaine inquired interestedly. "Thrudd Banner's quite famous, you know."

"He called her sweetheart."

"I think newspaper people use endearments quite casually, you know, Eric. Like in the theater world. Darling this and precious that," Mrs. Blaine said wistfully. It had been a long time since the once demonstrative Miss Nuttel had said anything of the kind to her.

"Take it from me, they are lovers. I saw the way she was clinging to his arm. And he was carrying a large envelope."

"It didn't sound as if they were going toward Sweetbriars. Perhaps to Dr. Wright's? Didn't I hear Sergeant Ranger's name mentioned?"

"You did. And I infer that they assume that he is being kept in the dark about something. Presumably by his superiors, with whom they are conspiring. So they're unlikely to be on their way to see him. I don't know where they're going, but I am quite certain of two things, Norah. First, that Forby and Banner are lovers as well as accomplices, and second, that they are involved in a criminal enterprise which has something to do with the contents of that envelope."

And for once, Miss Nuttel was absolutely right.

chapter

–19–

Sir Hurbert Everleigh made a steeple of his hands, arranged them in what looked vaguely like an attitude of prayer under one of his chins, and gazed at Delphick over the top of his glasses. "Don't ask me, Oracle," he said. "All I can tell you is what the commissioner in his infinite wisdom thought fit to impart to me: namely that Mr. Justice Thumper returned from Kent to his London residence yesterday morning, and that on arrival he telephoned to seek an urgent personal meeting with him. Though he had as always many other pressing claims upon his time, which of course costs the taxpayers even more than yours and mine, the commissioner received him for a few minutes that same afternoon. As a consequence of that interview, our master has had what he describes as a quiet word on the telephone with the chief constable of the county of Kent."

"Who is no doubt saying much the same thing at this moment to Chief Inspector Brinton as you have been saying to me, sir."

"That is not only entirely possible, but highly probable. Knowing that you two are as brothers, I'm quite sure that Brinton will be on the line to you presently to compare notes. Or you to him. Ever heard the expression 'wheels within wheels'?"

"I have, sir."

"Mysterious phrase, come to think of it, but one knows more or less what it means."

"Quite. In this context for some reason it puts me in mind of other handy idioms, such as 'old boy network', sir."

"It does indeed, Delphick, it does indeed. You're doubtless recalling that Sir George Colveden is not only a respected member of the Bench at Brettenden Magistrates' Court, but also often plays golf with the said chief constable. So it is safe to assume that the commissioner's call is unlikely to have come entirely as a bolt from the blue. Just between ourselves, who or what do you think persuaded Thumper to change his mind so dramatically between the time you left him that afternoon and the following day when he begged the commissioner to call the whole Parsons thing off? Apart from the burglary charges, of course."

"I very much wish I knew."

"Perhaps I should have mentioned that the commissioner told me that when they met, Thumper appeared to be acutely embarrassed. Admitted indeed that were it not a matter of some urgency, and the circumstances such that he wished the commissioner to be in no doubt about his identity, he would greatly have preferred to make his request by letter or telephone. Tell me, did Thumper seem to be more or less his usual unlovable self when you interviewed him at Rytham Hall?"

"Hardly that. In the first place he'd caught the father and mother of all colds in the head. He was wrapped up in an extraordinary dressing gown that looked a bit like a horse blanket, and got through half a box of Kleenex in about twenty minutes."

"It just goes to show that elderly gentlemen of sedentary habits shouldn't go for dips in lakes. Even at Glyndebourne. I see. So understandably he was a bit down in the mouth. But you say the famously unbending upholder of the law was nevertheless very much in evidence."

"Not exactly, sir. He struck me as being not only thoroughly under the weather, but also somehow chastened. In spite of being doggedly insistent that Parsons should be brought to account for sending him the threatening letters. Naturally I asked him what he thought about his daughter's decision not to press assault charges in respect of the incidents at the Hurlingham Club and at Glyndebourne."

"And?"

"He simply muttered something about his daughter being under much too much pressure before Wimbledon to concern herself with such things. She's due to play at Hastings tomorrow, by the way. The American girl who beat her at the Hurlingham Club last week."

"Well, judging by Ranger's report on her set-to with those two chaps at Glyndebourne, she seems to be in cracking form. Let's hope she wins this time. Is Ranger back here yet? Kent police have called off the protection arrangements, and it sounds as if there's little need for him to stay in Plummergen now."

"On the contrary, sir. He's getting married there tomorrow afternoon. To the local doctor's daughter." Delphick coughed modestly. "I am to assist at the ceremony."

"Indeed? In what capacity, may I ask?"

"Until this morning, it was to have been simply as a friend of the groom. But then Ranger rang me in something of a state, saying that his brother, who was to have been his best man, has just broken his leg water-skiing and can't be on parade. He asked me if I would consider helping him out. I was surprised to learn that he's a wine merchant, in Tewkesbury, of all places. The brother."

"I don't see anything odd about the idea of selling wine in Tewkesbury. Prosperous little place, he probably does quite well. Anyway, you have obviously been flattered into accepting."

"But of course. I'm pretty ancient to play best man, but—"

"I hope very much that Mrs. Delphick has consented to this reckless idea. My dear Oracle, do you realize what it means? A stag night out with the flower of young Plummergen manhood tonight? And tomorrow, the risk of mislaying the ring? A joky speech at the reception? Indiscriminate kissing of bridesmaids? Good gracious, I do envy you!"

The moment he saw Trish emerge from the changing rooms, Nigel shot up from the bench on which he had been whiling away the time by carving a heart transfixed by an arrow, with the penknife he'd carried on him since boyhood. Rushing to her side, he beamed at her and seized the large shoulder bag containing her gear.

"The car's just over there, darling Trish. Well, how did it go today?"

"Not bad. Not bad at all. My coach says he'll slaughter me if I don't beat Nancy this time."

"Gosh, I do think you're fantastic. After what you've been through this week, nobody would have blamed you if you'd pulled out of the match tomorrow."

"That would have been a jolly feeble thing to do. Besides, I feel fine. Never better. Don't bang my bag about, there's a pet." She watched while Nigel eased it into the space behind the two seats of the MG, and then slid into the car herself. Just as Nigel was about to start the engine, she reached over and put a hand on his wrist. "Don't I get a kiss?" Then, a couple of languorous minutes later, "Mmm, that's better. Off we go then, and drive nice and slowly. I want to feel lazy. You know, I rather miss the police escort, but at least we get a bit more privacy this way, don't we?"

"Police escort? Whatever—?"

"Dear Nigel, you're a rotten actor. Do you really think I didn't notice the plods following us every day? Honestly, I don't know why everybody takes one look at a girl with a few muscles and immediately assumes she must be thick in the head, too. I knew more or less what you were all up to from day one. And Mummy told me she'd known about the anonymous letters from the first, too."

"She did? But neither of you were supposed to! It was all to be a deathly secret, even that you were staying with us!"

"Which is why you went barging about the village telling everybody you met, I presume. Of course Mummy knew, but she was too frightened of my tyrannical old father to say so. Until going to Glyndebourne changed her life. Once she saw him go into the lake, and then the way he looked so terrified, clutching pathetically at that rather dishy man with the pink cummerbund who fished him out, well, I ask you!"

"Rather dishy? What an extraordinary thing to say. Especially as the blighter you see fit to describe as rather dishy is under arrest for conspiring to kidnap you."

"No, he isn't. Well, he's still in jug I think, but only for nicking the church silver. Miss Seeton and I put a stop to all the other nonsense. Wasn't easy getting my father to see reason, mind you, but in the end we got by with a little help from our friends." Trish hummed a snatch of the Beatles song and smiled enigmatically.

"What friends? You don't mean Mel and Thrudd, do

you? Why *did* they drop in unexpectedly yesterday evening, wanting to see him privately?''

''Can't imagine.'' Trish broke into a fit of giggles, and it was a little while before she could continue. ''You never know, perhaps they wanted his photo for the *Daily Negative*. Anyway, don't be cross. You're much dishier than the man in the cummerbund. And Mummy's a totally different woman. She was on the phone even before they left for London this morning, booking herself a beauty treatment at Claridges and a first-class stateroom on the Queen Elizabeth II. She's off to do some shopping in New York next week.''

''Is she really? Well, good for her . . . but I say, what's going to happen about—''

''Father? Oh, do him good to fend for himself for a while. Give him a chance to meditate on the error of his ways. Everyone's been getting at him, but it's only his vanity that's really hurt, you know. That and the fact that Colveden Senior gave him a jolly good talking to, according to Mummy. Told him he was a rotten bully and a disgrace to the old school. Quite right, too. You know, Nigel, I really think that must have got through to him. When he said good-bye to me this morning, he snuffled a bit—''

''Not surprised, he's got a stinker of a cold.''

''Don't interrupt. No, I mean he went a bit soppy, apologized for not having been a better father, and promised to try to improve in future. Even told me he loves me. First time in my life he's ever come out with anything like that. He could have fooled me all those years. Honestly, it was dead embarrassing, I can tell you.''

''Must have been. Oh Trish, I am going to miss you after this weekend. I wish I could be with you during Wimbledon fortnight.''

Trish threw back her head and gave herself up to warm,

full-hearted, infectious laughter. "Fortnight?" she managed to splutter eventually. "You must be kidding! Darling Nigel, I'm not a bad tennis player and I plan to get a lot better in the next two or three years, but if I get into the second round it'll be a surprise, and a miracle if I last into the third. After which my services won't be required. And your lovely ma and pa have already invited me back. So don't go chasing any other girls for at least a week, okay?"

"Tween yoonme," Bob Ranger said owlishly to his superior, "got admit tried Nige first." He pointed an unsteady finger at the young man in question, who was standing at the bar a few feet away, deep in conversation with PC Potter, Mr. Jessyp the headmaster of the village school, and Martha Bloomer's husband Stan. Potter was overawed by the honor of having been invited to a gathering of the notables of Plummergen, being modest by nature, and the presence of horny-handed Stan Bloomer was something of a comfort to him.

"And why not? Fine young man." Delphick wasn't anything like as tight as the bridegroom, but more than mellow enough to take a charitable view. He caught the eye of Thrudd Banner, who was sitting with them, and they exchanged winks while Bob sat back and nodded his head a good many times.

"Coon make it, though. Gotter go Trishtings with Hash. Hashtings with Triss." He peered anxiously into Delphick's eyes.

"Not offended?"

"Not a bit of it. Glad to oblige. Any time."

"Damn silly things, stag parties, don't you think?" Thrudd inquired. "Bob here would much rather be with Anne than brooding into his glass, and half the others aren't really eligible, anyway. Isn't it supposed to be all the groom's bachelor buddies that gather round to help him say good-bye to the single state?"

"Perfectly right. But I'm married, Potter's married, Bloomer's married. Don't think the schoolmaster is though. Nigel's a bachelor, and so are you, come to that."

Bob Ranger looked blearily from one to the other, and then himself winked with deliberation at Delphick. "Not long now," he then said. "Cording to Missessess. Weddin bells f'rim soon, too."

"Rubbish," Thrudd said at once.

"Who's the lucky girl, Thrudd? Not Mel, by any chance?" One look at his face was enough to tell Delphick that he had hit the jackpot. "Well I'm blowed! Congratulations!"

chapter
–20–

IT WAS a busy Saturday morning for a good many of the residents of Plummergen, and for all of the visitors temporarily housed there; except for a Dutch anthropologist and her engineer husband, who were on a bicycling holiday and had taken a room at the George and Dragon the previous evening. As sophisticated Hollanders they were naturally fluent English speakers, who had listened with fascination to snatches of conversation in the saloon bar, and correctly interpreted the status of the huge young man at the center of the ill-assorted but all-male group of revellers.

After they had enjoyed watching the entire ensemble, including the immensely respectable-looking older gentleman, join in a ragged but spirited performance of ''Knees Up, Mother Brown'', the anthropologist had jotted down for subsequent analysis a phonetic transcription of the incomprehensible words of what had to be a ribald bucolic song sung by Stan Bloomer. Then (tactfully in Dutch) she wondered aloud to her husband whether she hadn't made a mistake in devoting years of study to the customs of the people of the island of Lombok in Indonesia when there were equally fascinating rituals to be observed so much nearer home.

Their pleasure had been crowned when, later, they saw Thrudd Banner tiptoeing with exaggerated caution from his own room to the one they knew to be occupied by the young woman they had met and spoken to briefly when settling in. Since it was next door to their own, they also gathered aural evidence that not all the English are as phlegmatic and undemonstrative as they are reputed to be.

Now, at eight-forty on Saturday morning, having managed to deal with most of the Full English Breakfast included in the price of their room, they had nothing to do except decide whether to remain in the village long enough to see the actual wedding, or to press on as planned to Dover where the husband, a lover of poetry, wanted to spend some time on the beach in homage to Matthew Arnold.

The other guests at the George and Dragon had more on their minds. These now included Bob Ranger, for everybody concerned was agreed that it would never do for the bride and groom to spend the night before the wedding under the same roof, much less to court bad luck by setting eyes on each other on the great day, until the moment when Dr. Wright piloted his daughter to Bob's side in church.

Contemplating his reflection in the looking glass in his room, Bob decided that he wasn't in such bad shape as all that. Slightly fragile, but nothing a hearty breakfast wouldn't put right. The beer and whiskey chasers had flowed freely with a good time being had by all, but his wedding-eve booze-up had been positively sedate compared with some he'd participated in, not to mention certain post-rugger match celebrations. As the local representative of the law, PC Potter had been obliged to remove himself, Nigel, Jessyp, and Stan Bloomer at closing time anyway, but the three of them staying at the pub could've legally gone on drinking as long as they liked.

Thrudd hadn't hung about, though, once he spotted Mel

pop her face round the door to the bar and blow him a kiss, and as soon as he'd gone upstairs it was obvious the Oracle was more than ready for bed. Good sport he'd been, though, joining in like that. That was a laugh, when poor old Potter had nearly had a fit, when he realized that as a humble village bobby he had to cross arms and hold hands with a detective chief superintendent to sing "Auld Lang Syne". He'd probably tell the story for years to come and bore the pants off everybody he knew. Anyway, all that was last night, and today was today. Wedding at half past twelve, reception in the banqueting room here at the pub, should be over by three at the latest, and then—whoopee!

A few yards along the corridor, Delphick was brushing the tailcoat of his morning suit. The creases it had acquired in transit had hung out nicely overnight, and he thought he would probably pass his wife's inspection when she arrived later in the morning, in the care of the Brintons who were to pick her up at Ashford Station.

While taking his bath and shaving, he had been musing about the funny way things have of turning out for the best sometimes. Had he been a religious man, rather than an agnostic who happened to love the language of the Book of Common Prayer and the King James Bible, he might have attributed Sir Wilfred Thumper's change of heart to the workings of divine providence. Even accepting for the purposes of argument that God moves in a mysterious way His wonders to perform, however, it was altogether too much to credit the Almighty with selecting Mel Forby and Thrudd Banner as His agents in this particular bit of malarkey.

For at a late stage during Bob Ranger's stag party, an exuberant Thrudd had drawn him to one side, and muttering something about showing him some dirty postcards, produced a little pack of contact prints, cut roughly to the same size. It might have been that, having captured likenesses of Bob with his mouth open looking stupid, and Miss Seeton with hands upraised in genteel horror, as well as the drama of Thumper's immersion in the lake at the hands of Harvey and subsequent rescue by the same, Thrudd merely wished to add to the innocent fun of the party.

What he actually did was make Delphick feel much as Pythagoras must have done when he first worked out the truth about the hypotenuse of a right-angled triangle. After seeing those pictures of Thumper, it was like taking candy from a kid to elicit from a high-spirited Nigel Colveden the information that yes, Mel and Thrudd had dropped in at Rytham Hall to have a chat with the old buffer the evening before Lady T. towed him back to London.

Q.E.D., as Pythagoras himself might have remarked had he known Latin.

"It's just as well we picked up your morning suit from London on Tuesday," Mel was saying in the dining room as she buttered her last piece of toast. "Bet you never thought you'd have to put it on again today. Nice of the Wrights to ask us to the wedding at such short notice."

"I hate weddings," Thrudd grumbled. Of all the participants in the stag party, he had the worst headache. "Why do people get married?"

"Darned if I know. The thought of marriage gives me the creeps."

Thrudd looked into her eyes. It suddenly struck him that it was a perfectly beautiful morning. "Does it really?"

"It sure does."

"Um, Bob was saying that Miss Seeton's guessed about us, Mel."

"Doesn't surprise me. She has X-ray eyes. Well, I don't mind if you don't. I expect she's rather tickled about the idea, but I certainly hope she's not kidding herself that I plan on marrying you, Banner."

"You don't?"

"Nope. *Nyet*. So it's no use your asking."

"Oh. Right. I won't, then."

"You might try to look just a wee bit disappointed, though. I suppose it could be fun to live in sin for a while, but on the whole I think we should settle for visiting rights in each other's places."

"Don't forget Anne's new passport, Arthur. You only have charge of it until they're married, so you must give it to her immediately after they've signed the register. Put it in your cassock pocket. It would never do for them to arrive at the ferry to Calais without it."

"Thank you, Molly. It had slipped my mind, you know. What with all the coming and going with the police, and the Archdeacon and everything. Whatever should I do without you?"

Miss Treeves sighed and readjusted her hat. "Heaven only knows. At least you don't have to worry about the Archdeacon anymore, not until the police return the silver, anyway. I've never seen a man so delighted as he was when he realized what a lot of money it's worth, not to mention what was stolen from the other two churches. Mark my words, he'll try to make you sell it. But I shall deal with him if necessary in due course."

"Eric, I *do* wish you wouldn't," Mrs. Blaine wailed, trying to keep up. "I understand how you feel—"

"I doubt it. If you did, you would see how appropriate it is that I should make my statement in the church itself, in the presence of the principal culprits and so-called responsible senior police officers from both the Kent and the metropolitan forces."

"But it'd be so *mean* to spoil everything for Anne Wright. It isn't as if it's her fault . . ."

Miss Nuttel stopped dead, turned on her companion, and withered her with a fierce smile. "If she chooses to ally herself with a man who seems to be constantly on hand to do That Woman's bidding, that is her affair."

They had almost reached the church when a despairing Mrs. Blaine played her last card. "They won't let us in, Eric," she said. "All the guests must already be inside, and look, there's a big hire car coming. It must be Anne and her father . . . they'll *never* let us in now—"

"Oh, yes they will," cried Miss Nuttel, approaching the open doors.

"Oh, no they won't, you frightful woman!" thundered Sir George Colveden, superb in his wrath as he barred the way. Even Miss Nuttel fell back before the figure in the impeccable morning suit, eyes flashing and moustache bristling.

"She's overwrought, Sir George," Mrs. Blaine faltered.

"Poppycock! The pair of you are nothing but confounded, malicious nuisances. Now be off with you, or I shall summon Constable Potter and give you in charge for breaching the Queen's peace!"

Miss Nuttel flung her head back and her arms out, and in a banshee voice screamed *"There is no justice!"* It was an impressive performance, generating enough decibels to startle the pigeons that lived in the church belfry. Several of them fluttered out and one scored a dead hit, right in Miss Nuttel's eye.

"Oh, it was such a *beautiful* wedding," Miss Seeton sighed contentedly. It was just after five and she was at

Rytham Hall, having been swept off there by her friends after the reception, for what Lady Colveden described as a cup of tea and a wind down. "Anne looked so radiant, and Bob cut a fine figure in his morning suit, didn't you think? Such a beautiful gray silk tie."

"Oh, rather. We had a lovely cry, didn't we?" Meg Colveden said. "I noticed you get your handkerchief out too when they were taking their vows, George, you sentimental old darling."

"Tommy rot! Speck of dust in my eye. Delphick did his stuff very efficiently, I thought. Witty little speech at the reception, too. Short and sweet. And Brinton there as well, must say the police rallied round splendidly."

"And Nigel, dear. Sending those two telegrams from Hastings and then ringing up to tell Mr. Delphick which one to read out at the reception."

"*Two* telegrams, Lady Colveden?"

"Yes. Just in case Trish lost. That one just sent love and best wishes."

"How thoughtful. Instead of—"

"What was it, TRISH WON A CUP TODAY BUT YOU TWO ARE THE CHAMPIONS LOVE AND BEST WISHES FROM US BOTH NIGEL. Neatly put. Good lad, Nigel. Proud of him." Sir George hurriedly pulled out his handkerchief and blew his nose vigorously. Then he cleared his throat.

"To change the subject, got a bit of news for you, Miss Seeton. Brinton passed it on at the reception. Charges against all three of those fellows been dropped, on condition the burglars do a hundred hours voluntary community service apiece. And the other chap, your Tintoretto character. Agreed to accept, what is it, one of these damnfool new words, psychotherapy? Think that's it. D'you suppose that's what he needs, Miss Seeton?"

"Not really, but it will do no harm provided he is allowed to keep his job."

"That's been taken care of. Employers have said he can."

"Good. Then I shall go to see him regularly, and try to persuade Trish to go with me. He'll like that. He misses his own daughter so much, you see."

Meg Colveden smiled. "Another cup of tea?"

"How kind, I should love one. Sir George, do forgive my curiosity, but what exactly was that disturbance outside the church just before the bride arrived?"

"That? Oh, just The Nuts up to their usual nonsense. Shooed 'em off the premises in double quick time. If they'd given any real trouble I'd have come and asked you to take your umbrella to 'em, but they got a message from on high instead, and made a strategic withdrawal, as we used to say in the army. In other words, they ran away."